"I confess I'm quite am... ✓ ... has done in her altogether colorful, carefully researched, and sharply styled book *Mary's Journal*. She has not only held to basic truths, she has allowed me to meet Mary herself, as I can certainly agree she really might have been. Believe me, this is no small feat!"

—EUGENIA PRICE, author of *Savannah*

"*Mary's Journal*, though an imaginative fiction, is written so graphically that it turns real in the reader's mind."

—LUCI SHAW, poet and author of *God in the Dark*

"Beautiful writing, creative ideas, and I enjoyed the sensitive flow of words that seemed to come from the heart of God's chosen, beloved Mary."

—author MARGARET JENSEN

"Imagination with the texture of truth. This journal is an extraordinary blend of tenderness and common sense, sunshine and shadows. Thanks to Evelyn Bence, the Holy Family comes alive for us today."

—KATHRYN LINDSKOOG, author of *The C. S. Lewis Hoax*

MARY'S JOURNAL

A Mother's Story

EVELYN BENCE

HarperPaperbacks
New York, New York
ZondervanPublishingHouse
Grand Rapids, Michigan
Divisions of HarperCollins*Publishers*

HarperPaperbacks   *A Division of* HarperCollins*Publishers*
10 East 53rd Street, New York, N.Y. 10022

A hardcover edition of this book was published in 1992 by ZondervanPublishingHouse, a division of HarperCollins*Publishers*.

Cover illustration by Joan Perrin Falquet

First HarperPaperbacks printing: December 1995

Printed in the United States of America

HarperPaperbacks, ZondervanPublishingHouse, and colophon are trademarks of HarperCollins*Publishers*

❖ 10 9 8 7 6 5 4 3 2

For John,
a tree planted by streams of water

Contents

Acknowledgments

Thank you,
   Evy Herr Anderson, who convinced
me to pull the Mary proposal out of a file
drawer and send it to . . .
   Bob Hudson, Zondervan editor who
purchased and pushed.

Thank you,
   Linda Woolsey, for sharing daughter
Hannah's quips, and
   Camilla Luckey, Elise Chase, and
Ila Anderson for their interest and prayers.

MARY'S JOURNAL

A Mother's Story

Introduction

Impossible, you say. Mary would never have kept a journal.

I will not argue with you. In her day our notion of journal writing was virtually impossible for anyone. A professional scribe writing on papyrus or parchment—using a reed pen and ink of soot and glue—could get down maybe one hundred words an hour, one hundred lines a day. (Though much of this book has been written at that speed, it is for reasons other than technology.)

And then Mary was a woman. Despite museum paintings that depict the angel interrupting Mary as she's quietly reading a (bound!) book, it was rare for a Jewish girl to know how to read and write. The Scriptures were likely hidden in her heart, memorized and repeated for the promise and comfort they afforded.

But what do we know about Mary? While Matthew focused on Joseph's angelic visitations and role in the Christmas story, Luke centered on Mary. And not once but twice Luke described her as a ponderer, the kind of woman who, if alive today, would keep a journal: The night of Jesus' birth, as the shepherds left the nativity, "Mary treasured up all these things and pondered them in her heart" (Luke 2:19). In a scene twelve years later, after Jesus had been lost in Jerusalem for three days, Luke reiterated his point: "[Jesus'] mother treasured all these things in her heart" (Luke 2:51).

And so I write, imagining myself pondering her

conception of her world, so different from and yet so similar to mine.

In a practical sense the task set before me is impossible: How can one begin to detail thirty years in 170 pages?

And so I've been faced with choices. The Gospels give highlights of fewer than ten of young Mary's days. I've filled in the remaining years, until Jesus leaves Nazareth, with undated entries that skim the surface of the time.

One "surprise" in these pages calls for an explanation. The Christmas story we've always heard describes Mary wrapping Jesus in swaddling clothes and laying him in a manger "because there was no room in the inn." As they well might, preachers and songwriters, playwrights and poets have long milked that phrase, *no room in the inn*, for apt meaning beyond Bethlehem: As Isaiah prophesied, "He was despised and rejected by men . . . he was despised, and we esteemed him not" (Isaiah 53:3).

There's no question that Luke's Gospel says "there was no room." But there is question about the noun usually translated as "inn." The Greek noun used here in Luke 2:7—*kataluma*—can refer to an "inn," but it has other meanings as well, and it is not the noun Luke used to describe the hostel for travelers frequented by the Good Samaritan (see Luke 10:34).

Luke used the noun in one other place, in Luke 22:11 where Jesus, making preparations for the Last Supper, says to his disciples, "Say to the owner of the house, 'The Teacher asks: Where is the *guest room [kataluma]*, where I may eat the Passover with my disciples?' He will show you a large upper room, all furnished" (verses 11–12, italics added).

Kataluma, according to Dr. Kenneth E. Bailey, professor of New Testament at the Near East School of Theology in Beirut, can have a number of meanings, including inn, house, or guest room. In an article, "The Manger and the Inn: The Cultural Background of Luke 2:7" (*Bible and Spade,* Summer/Autumn 1981), Bailey defends this translation of the circumstance of Jesus' birth: Mary laid him in a manger because there was no room in the guest room.

This may make no sense to us Westerners, but it makes perfect sense to Palestinians whose lifestyle has changed little in two thousand years. Bailey explains the scene: The ordinary village peasant house was what we would call a split-level. The family lived on the larger upper level consisting of one room—or possibly two, the second being a guest room.

At night the family's animals were brought in to the small lower level for two good reasons: to guard against theft and to make use of their body heat, an extra shield against the cold nights, especially in winter.

In the floor of the upper level, just inches from the four-foot drop-off, one or more mangers were dug—troughs at just the right height to feed the animals, maybe a donkey or cow, domiciled for the night.

And there, in the corner of a crowded, caring household, Jesus might well have been laid in straw. As the angel told the peasant shepherds who no doubt laid their own newborns in mangers: "This will be a sign to you: You will find a baby wrapped in cloths and lying in a manger" (Luke 2:12). The word: He is one of you. One of us.

As is Mary, his mother, whom Catholics venerate and Protestants ignore, maybe fear, lest she cast a shadow near her son, lest homage to the mother edge out worship of the Savior.

My hope is that this fictional journal will prompt readers, Protestant or Catholic or neither, to reconsider Mother Mary: human and holy, worthy of wonder, respect, and acclaim.

I turn again to Luke for insight into Mary and her place among the heavenly cloud of witnesses that watches over our earthly comings and goings. Inspired with prophetic insight Mary's Magnificat includes this line: "From now on all generations will call me blessed" (Luke 1:48). Yet Luke 11:27–28 puts her glory in a different perspective:

> As Jesus was saying these things, a woman in the crowd called out, "Blessed is the mother who gave you birth and nursed you."
>
> He replied, "Blessed rather are those who hear the word of God and obey it."

If we esteem Mary it should be because she heard and followed God's call on her life—trusting Him with her present and future.

The idea for this book grew from a paragraph of a Sunday sermon preached by my pastor, Nicholas Lubelfeld. It may have been Epiphany Sunday; neither of us remembers the context, but he made mention of Mary in Egypt, waiting, not understanding the dark present—exile. She lived those years on hope, not knowing the end of the story.

For several years I'd thought my next book would be about *waiting*. But books are not books until words find their way to paper. The ideas that simmered in my mind never got served up, from the pot to the plate. There were several reasons for this but one was the lack of a framework on which to present the ideas; there was no rimmed plate that would keep the peas from rolling around the table.

But the life of Mary provided a frame to work within. And once I had the frame of her life before me, the manuscript no longer was focused on or confined to the subject of waiting, though waiting, I find, is traditionally a primary component of a woman's life.

When I focused on Mary, I saw a woman for all seasons, all generations. A daughter breaking away from her parents. A young wife concerned that she please her husband. A young mother questioning her ability to raise her children. A widow mourning the joy of her youth. An older mother forced by time to let go of her children.

Though I have tried not to violate the culture of her day, I have envisioned Mary as a mother not all that different from a modern woman, you or me. Laughing. Crying. Prodding. Sighing. Reaching. Watching. Yes, waiting. Waiting for a full redemption described by many beautiful images throughout the Scriptures.

Though Mary would not have been familiar with the image used by the apostle Paul, it is the one I leave with you, as a promise of things to come: "Now we see but a poor reflection as in a mirror; then we shall see face to face. Now I know in part; then I shall know fully" (1 Corinthians 13:12).

I look forward to that day, when I will see and know my Redeemer—the King. But I also hope to get acquainted with the highly favored woman chosen to be the Queen Mother.

Evelyn Bence
September 10, 1991

Mary treasured up all these things and
pondered them in her heart.

—*Luke 2:19*

PART 1

Conceptions

Every face turned to him grows
brighter and is never ashamed.

—*David, the psalmist*

What have I done to deserve this?

Blessed among women. Chosen.

My womb will bear . . . the promise . . . the king.

I believe the man I saw, the words I heard.

Understand them? Hardly. I can name others more worthy than I—like Mother. She's the mother of my faith, the one who's taught me what God requires, the one who deserves the favor I've found, and yet she's seen only daughters survive these years.

I know what I saw and heard but will she—who has not seen with her own eyes—believe my testimony?

So I told Mother about the man and his message. She wanted a full account: While she was laying out laundry to dry on the roof, a man looking ordinary except for the sheen of his skin appeared here in the house—just appeared, standing by the side of the loom. It wasn't like a dream; it was real.

Well, one thing was like a dream—a bad dream: I tried to scream but couldn't because my throat locked up. But that was just for a few seconds. "Rejoice. Don't be afraid, Mary." When he said my name—the way he said it—the scream died. I could listen.

"You are favored among women." He spoke in the Lord's name and said I would have a son—whom I'm to name Jesus. A king, he said, over Jacob's house.

It sounded so imminent, and my marriage still far off . . . How . . . ?

"The Holy Spirit," he said, ". . . the Son of the Most High."

As if it were a sign, he told me that barren Elizabeth is six months along: "Nothing is impossible with the Lord," he explained, hesitating as if waiting for an answer.

"I am His servant," I answered. "Let it be as He says." There seemed no other suitable response to his presence.

He left just as he'd come. No doorways. No eagle wings. In a blink he was gone.

Mother believed me in that she knew I wasn't lying to her. But she'd heard nothing. Seen nothing. She checked my forehead. Did I have a fever?

She was at the same time nearly overcome with excitement and praise and hope that the Lord had visited us (and to her it was as if He'd visited *us*, my favor being her favor) and with apprehension.

She clucked around for a while and then got very practical about the whole matter: Time would determine the truth. "Others have made claims, Mary." Was she scolding me?

Later she said she had a plan. Leah and Thomas are going to Jerusalem, leaving tomorrow. I should travel with them to visit Elizabeth. If the message is true and she's expecting, I should stay on; at her age she'll need help. If it isn't true, then that's that, and I should come back with Leah and put these visions out of my mind.

Mother said that she would speak with Father, but that I should tell no one else about any of this. No matter what the circumstances, these things—

babies—are women's secrets until there's no doubt. She was adamant. Was it because of her lack of faith? Maybe, though I think more a lack of faith in my youth than in the Lord. Mothers always seem so skeptical, convinced that old age is the price one pays for wisdom.

I really can't tell. Is she the wisest of all women—or the weakest in faith?

This evening she kissed me on the forehead and said, "If it's of the Lord, as you say, it will be well."

Yeah, I think she believes—or at least she hopes . . . and prays.

I cannot let myself think about the message for myself—until I find out whether or not the news of Elizabeth is true. I know what I have seen and heard and felt. But her miracle—bearing a child when she's as withered as old Sarah—will substantiate my hope of blessing. Blessing. Favored among women. Chosen.

I can hardly keep myself from telling Cousin Leah about the messenger, but Mother made a point of saying I mustn't.

This trip is taking too long. My spirit wants to break away from the group and run ahead, down, down, down, to the doorway of Zechariah and Elizabeth.

I believe. Let her blessing hail mine.

My soul praises the Lord.
My spirit rejoices in my Savior,
who has seen the willing heart of His servant.

It's true. But the story gets even more incredible, as a messenger also visited Zechariah and told him that dry Elizabeth would conceive. I want to know all the details of his encounter, but he was struck dumb in the ordeal and still has no voice, though Elizabeth is as talkative as ever—and the minute she saw me she knew of my favor. Her blessing lingers with me.

> *From now on all generations will call me blessed,*
> *for the Almighty has done great things for me.*
> *Praise to the holy Name.*
> *His mercy spreads over those who fear Him,*
> *from generation to generation.*

As I ran into their house, her child quickened as if even he rejoiced in our deliverance.

> *He has pulled down rulers from their thrones.*
> *He has lifted up the humble.*
> *The hungry He has filled with good things.*
> *The rich, sent away empty.*

I will stay and help Elizabeth as much as I can.

Zechariah was told to name their son John: the Lord is gracious, indeed.

Per my agreement with Thomas, we'll meet them tomorrow and tell them that I'll not return with them. Through Leah I'll send word to Mother about Elizabeth —and Zechariah.

He came. Have I known the Most High as the prophets did? Was the fire like the coals on Isaiah's tongue? Does my face glow like Moses'? Or is this something different? Some knowledge only a woman could be given?

In the night I lifted my soul in praise to the Most High and a power burst upon me, within me. I saw nothing. Heard nothing. Felt no hand touch me—but a fire that burned head to toe. There was no pain. I just melted—from ice to vapor in an instant. For a brief second I was consumed in a glory that belongs to another world.

Was this the making of a king?

I quickly see why the young bear the young. Elizabeth's body is worn and she tires long before the end of the day. Though her feet painfully swell and she must stop to catch her breath, I haven't heard one word of complaint. Before I arrived she sang a solitary song, praising God for lifting the sorrow of her years. Now we sing together, praising Him for His mercy.

> *He has come to the aid of His servant Israel,*
> *being merciful, according to the promise,*
> *to Abraham and his descendants forever.*

Zechariah in silence walks in and out. It's hard to know what he's thinking though his mood is not sour.

When Zechariah has something on his mind, he goes out in the backyard and writes messages with a stick in the sand. As soon as they're read by the appropriate person, he smooths them out with the sole of his sandal and often starts over.

With no explanation he'll leave the premises for

hours at a time. Elizabeth says he finds a few square yards of sand and carries on business almost, not quite, as usual.

Sand—the keeper of so many secrets.

I should have started bleeding earlier this week—but didn't. All of a sudden my future is a haze. What was I thinking? A real baby delivered in real time will cause real complications. If I *am* with child, as the messenger said, as Elizabeth's spirit and mine confirm . . .

I've been caught up in the surprise and hope and joy and just now imagine the trials of Joseph, or, rather, the trials of Mary. Elizabeth may believe my story—because she's received a miracle of her own. But who else is going to believe it? (That's why Mother told me to tell no one? I did tell Elizabeth everything, though she already seemed to know.)

Will Dad believe it? I don't know how much Mother told him. Did she tell him only the message about Elizabeth and that I was leaving to see if there was any truth in it? Or did she also tell him the word about me? Was Mother thinking ahead more than I was then—calculating the consequences of this? What *are* the consequences?

Today Zechariah clapped his hands, beckoning me outside to read his scrawls: "Do not be afraid. Your prayer has been heard. Gabriel." He made hand signs: Gabriel's message to him was also for me.

He then scrunched up his forehead so the furrows

were deep. He pointed to my forehead, and then with his fingers he smoothed out his brow, erasing the lines as he erases words in the dirt.

Dear Zechariah, thank you for your reminder . . . "Do not be afraid, Mary, you have found favor with the Lord."

Favor with the Lord—the Provider of manna, the Refuge of David, the Mighty who still hears and answers . . . Elizabeth's prayer, my prayer, Israel's prayer.

My prayer. Has a day ever passed that I have not prayed—that my womb would be blessed to bear the anointed one? Now my eyes, my spirit, my body—all agree that I have been favored of all women. For this captive generation I praise the Most High.

Yet in these secret pages and before the Name I admit that this, a wombed child claimed by no man, is not the answer I had in mind.

God of favor grant me favor with Joseph, a good man who will not violate Your law. Prepare his ears and his heart as You did mine and Mother's and Elizabeth's.

Joseph's family—aunts, uncles, cousins—all live down here in Judea, Bethlehem. Not all that far. At least one uncle, his father's older brother, is also a carpenter. I've heard Joseph say they trade back and forth sometimes. If one gets a windfall of wood or . . . well, I don't really know how it works. Someday I hope to know the ins and outs of the carpentry business, as much as a woman is allowed into the affairs of men. Anyway, I wonder if there's any chance of him showing up at the door here.

From my tightly woven spirit I can hardly pull up one thread that's dyed with desire to go home.

I talked with Zechariah today. The holy men have always understood that the Messiah would be born in Judea, not in Galilee. The question: Am I to maneuver myself to be in the right place at the right time?

Let's say I just stayed here and didn't go home. Word of my condition would spread. The trials would fire up. Joseph would arrive eventually, doubly shamed with desertion compounding my swollen belly.

No, I must go home and face Joseph and his deep-set Judean eyes. If he sends me away—with or without the trial of bitter waters—I can return here. That will get me back onto this land the Lord loves more than our lowly Galilee.

Zechariah said I may return to his house—any time for any reason. But then he ended our conversation by sand scratching, "But wait on the Lord. Who knows His ways?"

Elizabeth's deliverance is near. She spends more of her days resting, even sleeping. I play my flute or sing the praises. She simply nods.

She says I must stay with her. I've never seen a human birth. I heard Leah's cries, screams actually. The curse of pain tortured by terror. I saw the hemorrhaging rags and the basins of debris. She told me it was a sword and a flame and a crushing rock—all at the same time. She said she had to fight off demons to hold onto the hope that she would hear any cry but her own. (Sneering death hovers over birth. How many of our Nazareth women have lost their breath while pushing out life?)

Elizabeth prays for mercy—and strength—and I assure her I will stand by.

A bloody boychild, as promised, with lusty lungs and lots of hair. I think Leah could not have suffered more than Elizabeth; was it Elizabeth's age that muted her cries—or was it the pressure she was pushing on my palms? Her nails pierced my left hand—then my right hand when I couldn't stand the pain anymore (as if my agony had been anything compared to hers).

What more could I do but wipe her brow and sing our favorite psalms? She kept asking for Psalm 67: May God be gracious to us and bless us and make His face to shine upon us . . .

I had told her I would stand by and yet (was it the sight? was it our exhausting push? was it my own condition?) I started to faint when she gave her last cry—which I vaguely remember sounding like a laugh.

The midwives did not need a third patient to tend.

I have wrapped my palms, and when Elizabeth woke from her sleep she asked me whatever had happened to my hands. Shared labor, I said.

I laid the bound and salted baby in her arms, and she unwrapped him as Zechariah looked on, curious and excited yet slightly detached as if this were a grandchild and not of his very own member. Maybe I just misread his silence.

We are surprised that Zechariah's tongue has not been loosened, as the messenger said the affliction would be temporary, lifted when the child was born.

Elizabeth's milk is not coming in—at least enough of it—and everyone is somewhat on edge. For such a little creature, the child has a fierce cry. The midwives are arranging for wet nurses, and Elizabeth has taken to dipping her finger in honey for him to suck.

Actually, Zechariah does it too. He may be dumb but he isn't deaf.

Just to see what would happen, when no one was in the room I gave John my dry breast. How long would he suck before losing interest? No fool him. One lick and he turned his head away.

For someone who can't speak, Zechariah has outdone himself in inviting the whole town to the circumcision feast. Of course the event is thirty years overdue.

Zechariah was ready to hire three women to bake enough bread, supplementing what we bake here. But each insisted on donating her time. To help serve, he will hire two day-laborers. This is going to be quite a celebration.

Praise to the gracious Lord who loosened Zechariah's tongue—and just as he was announcing John's name to the guests, skeptical of Elizabeth's word.

Praise to the gracious Lord who anointed Zechariah with words fit for the whole nation:

> *And you, my child, will be called*
> *a prophet of the Most High,*
> *for you will go before the Lord*
> *to prepare the way for Him,*
> *to give His people the knowledge of salvation*
> *through the forgiveness of their sins,*
> *because of the tender mercy of our God,*
> *who will hang the rising sun above us*
> *to shine on those who live in darkness . . .*

But before that he talked of another, a horn of salvation in the house of David, sent to rescue us from the hand of our enemies, to give us strength to serve the Lord without fear . . .

When his eyes were not raised toward heaven, they rested on me, as if to reinforce a verbal blessing:

> *Praise be to the Lord, the God of Israel,*
> *for He has visited His people to redeem them.*

We all agree that I must return home now as soon as we can find a traveling party. In the excitement of the birth my own story has seemed faraway and dreamlike. If I could just stay here and hide inside the safe boundaries of Zechariah's property . . . have no contact with the outside community. If I could just dig a hole in the ground—like a mole?—and never come out. If I had wings like a dove, I could fly away.

Enough of this.

I think I'm going to be sick at my stomach.

Zechariah gave me a letter he has written to Father. Though I didn't ask to read it, I did ask what it says: It tells his story—his visitor, his silence, his son—and his confirming word about the child in me.

As I left, his last words were, "May Joachim believe—and Joseph, also."

Last night we sang songs late around the fire, though I fell asleep long before anyone else. We slept under the slivered moon.

I've always looked forward to the new-month calendar campfires that flicker like stars on the hills from one horizon to the other. Remember Father counting the days, looking at the sky, and trying to guess (will this month have twenty-nine days? thirty?) the decrees of the Jerusalem stargazers who set off the chain of signal fires, starting on the Mount of Olives. The silent word: A new month has begun.

How I'd beg Father to take us out to the cliff to see the calendar fires. When there, he'd praise the Name for the new beginning and pray a month's blessing on his house.

Now here we are again at day one. And before nightfall I will walk into Father's house and tell Mother my news. I thank the Name for Zechariah's letter. Zechariah's neighbors would not believe Elizabeth's word, simply because she was a woman.

And the nontraditional naming of a child is hardly on an even plane with this nontraditional conception.

Lord, turn soft the hearts of men not known for their mercy toward women. Hear my prayer for blessing on my house.

PART 2

Explanations

Vindicate me, O Lord, for I have led a
blameless life.

—*David, the psalmist*

The minute Mother saw me she looked me over and knew of my condition, yet the first thing she asked was about Elizabeth's. Had she delivered safely? And a boy? And Zechariah, had he regained his speech? What did they make of all this?

Then suddenly, when I was in the middle of a sentence, she lost interest and turned her attention to me. "And you." Was it an accusation or a question?

"Yes, Mother, as the angel said . . . No one touched me." Did I sound defensive?

"Mary, my ears want to hear your news. I want your blessing to be my blessing. But your father—and Joseph. What are we going to tell Joseph?" (Hadn't her faith for our well-being been stronger when the "storm" had been but a small cloud on the horizon?)

And who walked in the door right then? Father and behind him eager Joseph, eyes dark and deep as I'd remembered. (News travels fast in this town. Trumpets might as well announce the comings and goings.)

We chatted of everyone's well-being, and in those first few minutes Joseph's mood changed. After his initial welcome, he grew temporarily sullen, even stern, displeased that I'd been away so long and with no direct explanation.

It seems Mother had told him I'd had a dream—a premonition of Elizabeth's condition. The explanation had appeased but puzzled him.

I now filled in a few details—an angel's visit when I was awake, not asleep. He had told me of two babies, Elizabeth's and a holy son that I would carry in my own womb. A holy son, Joseph.

O Lord, I could not say that the child *is*. I spoke in the past and indefinite future, not in the present.

He stayed for dinner and quickly loosened up and was laughing with Dad. Two happy—blessed—men, knowing half a blessed story.

I do like him. There's so much to hope for, so much to gain—or lose.

When he left you could hear him whistling, far down the street. A sure sign that he's happy.

We soon readied the beds. I took my cues from Mother, who didn't scold or praise me. "Tomorrow morning," she whispered. "Your father has to know."

So I have another night to pray for tender mercies.

My God, are You here? Now?

Such accusations. Adulterer. Liar. Conspirator. (How dared I deceive old Zechariah, obviously crazed?) The worst accusation of all—blasphemer—I'm sure it was on his tongue the moment he just stared at me: "No. No. I cannot say the word." He tore at his beard and yelled at Mother. For sending me to Judea. For spinning a web of such a story . . .

Then he came back at me and started over again, more arrows of accusation. How could I do this to him? "Have I endured this town's laughter for ten straight years—because I spent my evenings teaching my younger daughter the law and prophets and alphabet as if she were a son—to get this thanks in return? Ah, you never knew of their scorn. How foolish of me to have protected you from that. And from the hard bargain Jacob dealt me—for you to wed such a pick of a man as his Joseph. Had I told you, you might have shown more gratitude and not spit in my face like this."

Why had I made up such a story? Had I lost my mind? Was I playing David on the run in Gath, feigning insanity to save my life? ("Not a very good job, Mary , and not very funny.")

"You've always been one for dreams—nightmares. Is this some game of your imagination?" . . .

If it's not Joseph's child, if I'm going to lie about whose child it is, why not just lie and say it *is* Joseph's? Why test Heaven's wrath by bringing His messengers into this.

Father. Father. I was wiping tears off my chin, yet I remained amazingly calm. I was Queen Esther walking the corridor toward her king. I was Daniel facing the lions. With reason, I kept holding out Elizabeth's miracle—Abraham and Sarah's miracle, a child in old age—as a guarantee of my miracle. I stood guiltless.

Dad started detailing his cold view of the facts: Joseph would think only one thing: adultery. There could be a trial . . . the disgrace . . . a divorce . . . the ruin of us . . .

Dad's anger finally turned into wrenching sobs that unsettled me more than his rage. We stood across the room from each other. On one side Mother and me crying, embraced in each other's arms. On the other side Dad collapsed on a stool. At first there were no words. Finally I said, "The messenger said that I was not to be afraid. Surely his word was assurance for all of us."

Dad soon left the house, heading out toward the

cliff. He didn't come back until long after dark, when Mom and I were in bed. I pretended to be asleep. Mom tried to talk to him but he just grunted and turned his face to the wall.

Dad started out the day grilling me: Who is the father of this child? He had rechanneled his anger away from me and to some son of a heathen swine. If someone had forced me, justice needed to be done. "You've always been kind, Mary, too kind. This is not the time for lies in the name of mercy. I want a name. Whom are you protecting? You think Joseph isn't going to demand justice?"

And he tore into Mother: "I can't believe you'd do this. Send her off to Zechariah's, thinking I'd never know, thinking some scheme could get us out of this mess. Crazy old Zechariah and Elizabeth conveniently cooperated, but I'm not going to buy into it."

I cried—and held my defense.

Dad: "If you're so determined that no one touched you, why are you so determined that you're with child? Have you felt life?" No. "Anna, can't a woman's cycle stop for months and start again when she's not carrying life?" Yes. "Can't a girl's belly swell when she's not carrying life?" Yes. "If you are so determined to hold to your story, Mary, we will not speak of this issue to Joseph until you have felt life. No more discussion."

With that he left for the pottery and I fell into Mother's arms.

At first Mother said we have no choice but to wait. She saw some wisdom in his words. If I claimed that no one touched me, the real test of life is the baby's quickening. If that never comes, we have risked my life and my dowry—for what?

But Mother, we know . . .

By afternoon she was agitated: It was a horrible idea, she said. If I waited that long everyone in town would be talking—to each other and to Joseph. His humiliation with our silence would be the end of the matter. We can wait, she figured, two weeks at the most.

Mother said we would pray for seven days—for the Lord's direction to be clear. Then we would decide what to do. In the meantime, I'm to stay as close to home as possible.

How is it that my glory has turned into my shame?

Since I've returned home, at the well Judith and Rebekah and Naomi have been full of laughter—and questions. Why did I leave town so quickly? I've told them that we had news of Elizabeth's baby. She needed help. But today Judith asked whatever was wrong with me. "This week you haven't let go of your mother's skirts. Did Joseph scare you away?"

"Of course not, you're crazy. I've never been away three months before. I missed her."

"Yeah, well you're a betrothed woman. You'd better get used to being out of her sight—or are you going to ask her to move in with you? Wouldn't Joseph like that . . ." She ran off with Rebekah and Naomi and left me standing there, hoping Mother hadn't heard all this but being quite sure she had.

Tonight Father quoted Jesus ben Sirach—for my benefit not for his: "The worry of a daughter keeps a father awake. When she's a child, he worries she will never marry. When she's married, that she does not please her husband. When she's a virgin, he worries that she will be defiled, left with child and in his own house. When she has a husband, that she will go astray. When she's married, that she will be barren.

"You have a headstrong daughter? Be sure she does not make you the laughingstock of your enemies, the talk of the town, the brunt of gossip, putting you to shame."

With that I saw the Lord crack open a door. I saw a way to touch Father's logic. I looked at Mother whose eyes told me I could speak: I will be the brunt of the whole town's gossip if we try to ignore this much longer.

He listened. Then he lay on the floor, turned his face to the wall, and put his cloak over his head. From where do I get the impulse—sometimes wanting to run away and hide from it all?

Vindicate me, O Lord, for I am blameless.

It started with a simple question.

Joseph: "Mary, are you well? You have grown heavy, as if you are carrying the weight of the world."

"Yes, I'm well." The smile is faint but genuine.

Mother takes us all off guard, cutting in with cold reality: "Mary is with child, Joseph. The holy child, as the angel told her. It's within her, though she hasn't been with a man."

Father stares at her.

Joseph stares at me. I nod yes.

He stares at Father who is as dumb as Zechariah and staring at me, not Joseph.

Father—was his look of love? Or fear? With so much at stake he couldn't confirm or deny my story. (If it's *not* true, then whose child is it and what will justice demand?)

Finally Father speaks: "So she says."

I tell my story, just as I'd told it before, adding the last detail—that the child has already been conceived—and by no man.

Ignoring that final phrase and weighing his words—negotiating my future—Father asks Joseph to stand up and claim this child if it be his.

Joseph gets red. His name and honor will not be smeared in this or any house , now or ever.

His anger I see and hear, but a faster arrow flashes from his eyes: Abel's fleeting last look at Cain. Trust betrayed.

Would a public trial, being forced to drink the bitter waters, be harder than this day?

My God.

His eyes.

My God, my sure defense. Mother says I've been giddy. I say I've been Miriam dancing on the east bank of the Red Sea, praising Heaven for a deliverance so grand that gratitude—and relief and surprise—can escape only through motion.

My God, my sure defense. Jehovah-jirah, the Lord will provide. Last night Joseph had a dream. The angel. When you've seen the messenger of the Lord you believe his word—and the word of others who have seen him.

There were tears in Father's eyes when Joseph said he wanted to go ahead with a private wedding—claim me and the child as his own. Dad grabbed my hands. "My dear one. My dear one," he repeated, in spirit tearing at his shirt, begging my forgiveness—or Heaven's.

I am yours. You are mine. Today the marriage covenant seems so much more drastic and trustworthy than before. For me—for the Most High—Joseph has risked the honor of his name. (Yesterday did he have a more highly prized possession?)

At a crossroads, he had two choices: (1) to walk away from me, abandoning me in (and) my shame; (2) to take my shame as his own.

I can see that his motivation was loyalty to the Most High, not to me. (Wasn't it Joshua's, "As for me and my house we will serve the Lord"?) And yet that loyalty to Heaven will bind him to me, true as a door to its hinge.

And my heart's bond to him? His choice—we are one at any cost—spins a cord that death will strain to break.

I have gotten a good man from the Lord.

Yesterday I was grateful for merely a husband, and right to be. Today how can I be so fickle—to mourn the wedding celebration I have been planning for how long? Since memory was born. Since I first smelled the fragrance of Cousin Leah's bridal joy.

Judith and Rebekah and Naomi—we won't spend a day laughing and primping and pinching, waiting for the sounds of Joseph's train, hungry for the feast to follow.

Come on. Let go. Is a big wedding party something to mourn when you've been plucked from a lapping fire?

A child—of my own. The one thing I've always wanted, though I haven't imagined it would come like this—at least since the day Mother told me that men seed women in the dark of the night.

A holy child. The one thing Israel has always wanted, though what rabbi would believe my story? How many other women have pushed sons from their wombs and then claimed secret knowledge: He's God's anointed one, sent for such a time as this—to deliver, to reign, just you wait and see?

And the generations waited. The boys grew to be elders who obeyed the commandments, said their prayers, raised their families, and died of old age. Or they became rebels who dreamed of revolution, schemed in dark rooms, rallied in market streets, and died as martyrs for a cause.

Their mothers would have done better to let truth justify itself, let Heaven reveal His plans for their children through some mouth other than their own.

I write this as if it's my own wisdom, when actually most of it is Mother's advice. She tells me—and Joseph—still never to speak of the messengers or messages.

I'm relieved not to have heard Joseph's conversation with his parents, though I will have to live with the results. Tomorrow I am to move under their roof until Joseph can find us a house to rent. The only thing he knows of is crazy Nathan's tiny cave, which I hear is piled with filth. (In Abraham's bosom may he have found the peace that eluded him here.) Surely we could fix it up quickly, to spare me living with a woman unprepared for my presence.

Father, Joseph, and Joseph's father, Jacob, talked to the rabbi today, to ask him to join our quiet wedding procession and bless our union.

Mother talked to me of a man's drawn sword, whispering assurances that the pain is short-lived. It's Heaven's way. Like the pangs of birth that must precede the joy of a squirming child. Hold on.

Exhausted tonight. Mother and I washed every piece of clothing I own that wasn't on my back. We scoured the house, as people will be stopping by. She sent me out to collect rockrose for perfume gum, while she spent every "spare" minute weaving, hoping in vain that she'll finish the table linen she's making for me.

Her last words tonight: "Mary, you are beautiful as any bride. Fair as Jerusalem. Bright as the noonday sun."

I felt so secure. Is it possible I'm still worried Joseph may change his mind?

Dream: It was my wedding night, a real wedding. Come dark, Judith, Rebekah, and Naomi left me inside under the canopy and went out to the front gate to welcome Joseph's party, delayed, delayed, later, later. The girls were giggling, as much for themselves and their own wedding nights as for me and mine.

Finally, in what seemed the middle of the night, I heard the young men coming. Above the music I heard Joseph whistling. But when he got to the gate he didn't stop, kept dancing right on down the street into the village. The girls were at the gate, but he didn't notice them. Their lamps weren't lit and they didn't hail him; they sat there as tongue-tied as Zechariah at the first sight of his unbound boy.

I woke up surprised and relieved that I was still sleeping under my father's roof, listening to his snore. To shake loose from the dream, I forced myself to wonder if Joseph will snore as loudly as Dad. Maybe he's too young. Maybe it grows with age, like hair on a man's chest.

Is it possible I'm still worried Joseph may change his mind? No, that's not it. I'm afraid I won't know how to wife him. I won't know what to do, like the speechless virgins in the dream.

Word has gotten out. Joseph's looking for a house, talking to the rabbi . . . Have you taken a good look at Mary since she came back?

Mother said she'd go alone to the well this morning, and she was quiet but testy when she returned. She threw herself into the chores; we've offered to make the cakes for tonight . . .

I should have asked her what happened at the well, but I didn't want to know and she obviously didn't want to tell me. I'll have to go myself, tomorrow or next week, and I'll find out soon enough.

As busy as she is she has sent me out of the work yard, here into the house, to "collect myself," to bathe and get ready. I wish she were less distracted, more present with me on my last day at home.

Leah is here, outside talking with Mother. I can't hear the words but can tell she's asking questions. I must go rescue Mother who is trying to rescue me.

PART 3

Gestations

You knit me together in my
mother's womb . . .
I was made in the secret place

—*David, the psalmist*

Will I be able to write in this house, in the company of so many strangers? The cast: Younger brother Joaz scorns Joseph with undisguised self-righteousness. The older siblings were pleasant enough last evening and are gone now. Little Mary (four) is just delighted with the excitement and my attention. If she weren't napping, she'd be here pulling on my skirt, asking what I was doing.

Mother Judith. Her Judean arrogance is oppressive. She wishes her husband hadn't dragged her up here to Galilee, and she wishes I hadn't been dragged so untimely under her roof. She wears an insincere smile, an ineffective mask that doesn't conceal her annoyance, if not disdain. Joaz blames Joseph. She blames me, as I surely connived and seduced her without-spot-and-blemish son.

If she only knew the half of her son's virtue: Last night we had the guest room, of course. They left us with their knowing winks. "We would have found you mandrakes, but you've done well without them . . ."

Once alone Joseph and I looked into each other's eyes and burst out laughing. Despite what his family, even the whole town, thinks, here we were for the first time ever in the privacy of each other's company.

The laughter dissolved into kisses that might have dissolved me had Joseph not broken away, deadly serious. He sat me down on a mat and whispered confidences he didn't want to leak through the curtain: He was—is—determined that we must not be one until after the child is born. There must never be any question about this child. In my mind. In his. There must be no interference, no hand but Heaven's.

He's right. It's as it should be, though it wouldn't have entered my mind. A bride who resists her groom is not a bride for long.

His hand running through my loosened hair, he awkwardly begged my help. Trembling, gulping, groping for words he spoke for fear of the Lord. We must walk a fine line, each giving the other the pleasure of warm company, without turning pleasure to pain—which he seemed right then to be suffering.

I suppose I should speak for myself only and not for him, but I feel so naive in these matters that I hardly know what he means about pain. I am happy just to sleep at his back, nestled under his cloak, waking with the songs of doves.

A blessing: Before he turned his back to me, Joseph repeated the dinnertime toast of his family, mine, the rabbi. Bethlehem's blessing on Boaz and Ruth: "May the Lord make the woman who is coming into your home like Rachel and Leah, who built up the house of Israel. May you prosper in Ephrathah and be famous in Bethlehem. Through the children the Lord gives you by this young woman, may your house be like the house of Perez, the son Tamar bore to Judah."

May the Lord indeed bless, as He already has.

Went to the well today. I didn't have to talk to anybody to know their thoughts: "How we misjudged

Joseph, thinking him a patient, temperate young man. But no, he's obviously ruled by his passions. And Mary, did she try to dissuade him? Did she encourage him? I never would have thought . . . Such a promising pair. Such a disappointment. A pity to poor Anna, her sons dead, her younger daughter a shame."

Judith didn't hold her tongue. "Taking off to help Elizabeth. Did you think you'd be able to run away from this?" She raised her hand, pointing in the general direction of my waist. "Mama's girl, huh? I should have guessed—Joseph's lady laid."

Naomi and Rebekah held back, waiting for my response, which came out, I fear, as a challenge: "Through the children the Lord gives Joseph, may his house be like the house of Perez. And you, Judith, may you bear your husband a quiverful."

They walked away. Or maybe I did, I don't remember.

The benefits of being newlywed and living in your in-laws' home: You have an exclusive claim on the guest chamber.

I got sidetracked and never finished describing the cast of characters in this house. There's also Father Jacob. Though it's an inconsequential matter, he walks, almost runs, rather like a mouse. Flitting head-first from chore to chore. (Would I have accepted Joseph's proposal if he had a similar gait? I fear not; Lord forgive my pride.)

He'll interrupt any conversation or task and can be a nuisance. But I must say he is the kindest, most generous heart here, excepting dear Joseph and little Mary. He does good work and is an honest man, so he has a steady business. His customers seem to overlook his idiosyncrasies.

This child came to life today, a flutter in my belly soon after I got up. Life!

And now I must wait. Five months of days followed by nights. Women since Eve have been waiting wrenching deliverance.

Will a child conceived of heaven be born of earth—in blood and pain? Or might I be spared? The messenger promised a son, nothing more about travail or its absence. If I think of the worst scenario, he did not say that I would live to know the joy of counting fingers and toes.

So now I must wait—and pray that I am delivered from the depths of Eve's curse.

I watch Joseph with his little-doll sister, Mary. She begs him to carry her on his shoulders, twirl her around as they both sing Miriam's "Horse and Rider." Well, he sings and she giggles.

He is tender with her, more than Joaz is. Joaz's impatience might be his youth, though I am not convinced of that.

Joseph walked in this afternoon with the key to Nathan's house dangling around his neck. Now it's just a no-small matter of cleaning it out. Don't we all bring the donkeys into the house at night? Keep them on the lower level. Safe from thieves. Their body heat a cloud of warmth on winter nights. But don't we all take them outside first thing each morning, even on the Sabbath, and clean the dirt from the floor?

Yes. But Nathan was not exactly one of us. His beast was his child and unspeakably unkempt. That lower level is caked to the elbow with foul straw.

Exhausted from cleaning out Nathan's mess. We evicted (I hope) a good-sized family of rats housekeeping in the manger. (How merciful our Creator if He can call such vermin good.)

Mother was such a Heaven-sent help. Back to her joyful self, picking up a song the minute the conversation ran dry. She astutely inquired as to the pain of our union and I astutely told her of Joseph's reasoning and restraint. She was surprised. Got an odd, fleeting look on her face, which I couldn't classify as grin or grimace.

Before we left tonight we strewed the floor with wild mint leaves and pine needles. Wonder if it will cut the smell, so overpowering today that I was actually glad to return here to eat under my mother-in-law's turned-up nose.

Tomorrow we must clean out the yard, Joseph helping with the hauling. The fig tree in the back is such a beauty. Shady and heavy with fruit.

Then, after the Sabbath, we'll be able to move in—or is it out?

We are in. The house is so small but we have so little to spread out. The two chests, Joseph's betrothal gifts. My grandmother's spindle and loom. Enough cups and dishes to get by on. A mill was left here, comes with the house.

The smell here is sweeter than it was last week.

Dream: Was cleaning out the lower level here, Mother and I sweeping mounds of straw toward the door. I went upstairs to our living level, to be above the hewn manger, so I could easily sweep the basin's debris down onto the lower floor. In a foolishly wild swoop I smacked the straw, sending dust and reeds flying up into my face. When my vision cleared I reeled backwards. I'd unsettled not rats but an angry coil of snakes, three or four, the largest hissing angry as a bear robbed of her whelps and snapping—at me . . . and this child.

I woke up. Shivers. Sat up. Shook Joseph. Asked him to pray with me, pray away the devils of the night.

"You will not fear the terror of the night, nor the pestilence that stalks in the darkness."

He is not totally at ease with me. Though a man brought up by a mother and with older sisters isn't oblivious to the ways of women, I am of course not the sisters he has known all of his twenty years. I am his wife yet a stranger. They can say what they want, but I never spoke to him in private until we were wed. (Now don't get defensive . . .)

And then the sexual estrangement, if that's what it might be called.

Maybe it's I who am not at ease with him—husband yet stranger. I am indebted to him and feel as if he must expect something of me in return. More than what I'm giving him. But what?

Combing out my hair this morning. In the looking glass I saw Joseph behind me, staring at me from across the room as little Mary would. A childlike fascination with the unfamiliar other: Who are you? How did you get here? What are you doing?

I turned around and he turned away self-conscious.

Yesterday, my first Sabbath as hostess in my own house, now properly blessed. Ten for dinner: the rabbi and wife, Mom and Dad, and the four of Joseph's family living at home. Someday we will have a proper table and stools. Now we sit on the floor, around the two chests, covered with the cloth Mother brought with her, having finished it since the wedding. She arrived at noon, as promised, with two wrapped fish in hand, eager for us to look as if we have our feet on the ground.

Joseph says my hand was shaky as I lit the Sabbath lamp at the sound of the trumpet blasting the official pronouncement: The Sabbath has begun to shine.

Lighting the lamp. Why must even this womanly privilege be tainted by the curse of Eve? Lest anyone forget that woman by her sin extinguished the light of man's soul.

It's always so: The weak blame the defenseless for their own faults.

But what do I have to give this child?

When I first asked myself the question my mind went blank. There will always be a demand for Joseph's carpentry. I expect there'll always be food on our table. But aside from the bare essentials, what do I have to give this child?

I'll start a list and add to it as I think of things.

What was it that my mother gave me?

I can give him:
  my womb
  my arms
  my years
  my example
  my laughter
  my song
That's it, I'll give him my song.

Today and yesterday as I worked—grinding, kneading, sweeping—I sang psalms as usual but not at all as usual. Instead of singing "to myself"—or to the Lord—I sang to him, to this child I carry. I want to think he goes to sleep to the sound of the lullaby that trickles down my throat.

Joseph quiet tonight. I asked him what he would have done if the angel had not given him the message. I don't think he wanted to answer, but he did, and honestly. He had gone to bed that night thinking he should give me a bill of divorcement without making accusations or demanding a trial.

Of course my soon-evident condition would have been a trial of its own. I expect Father, still distrusting

my word alone, would have sent me off. Down to
Zechariah's? For how long? A year? Five? Would a
son and I have been welcomed back?

I smiled at Joseph, again grateful that this shameful
glory is ours, not simply mine.

Being a mother's daughter and being a wife—not
the same thing. Though I, more than she, carried the
water, gathered dung cakes, kindling, and fire-
wood . . . , I was ultimately not responsible for the
whole household, the day's womanly chores, dawn to
dusk: hauling, scrounging, spinning, weaving, firing
the stones, grinding the flour, baking the bread, gathering the figs . . . the list!

I must do it all before evening, and if I slow down
and start to dawdle (as Mother would call it) there's
no one to fuss at me. Move along. The sun is walking
faster than you are.

Tonight Joseph came in for dinner and it wasn't
ready, the lentils still lumps in the miry brew, which
I'd grossly overseasoned with the wild rosemary I
was so proud to have found this morning while
"dawdling."

I was obviously flustered with this treat-turned-
disaster, and Joseph was trying to say the right thing.
"It doesn't matter. We can eat late and—I like rosemary just fine."

But I knew it did matter. He's told me he likes to
eat right when he gets home, and, come on, eating
that stew would have called for fortitude on anyone's
part.

Anyway, I burst into tears, which he didn't understand and I couldn't explain, though now, writing it

out, the reasons are clearer. When two people are trying so hard to please each other, how can it suddenly all turn to muck?

He's done this several times now: About the hour all honorable people go to bed, he gets unusually quiet and agitated. Mumbling something I never quite understand, he leaves the house. The first few times I think he didn't leave the yard, but last night I'm sure he did. Was gone a long time. I went on to bed, and when he came and lay down with his back to me I pretended to be asleep, as I think he hoped I would be.

Each of the stars in the black sky is a prayer to my Lord for my love.

This morning I reached for Joseph's hand and had him feel this boychild, banging like a drummer announcing the dawn. It seemed to surprise—and delight—him, that I am carrying around so much carryings on.

He is of course very aware of this child, the blessings and complications it—he—affords us. But, alas, not half as much as I, the wombed one.

I am getting big, which means I have to make better progress on the new dress I'm making for myself, as I must be ready to tear up the worn one for swaddling. This little one must be bound tight in a womb of cloth, secure against the night through which the devils fly.

He's talking about moving to Judea. Leaving. Taking all we own with no provision for coming back for more than brief visits.

Am I being punished for—just weeks ago—writing too assuredly? Not humbly acknowledging our dependence on the Lord? Claiming there would always be demand for Joseph's trade?

Tonight, out of the clear blue, he says that work has slackened off since we've wed. (He was choosing his words so carefully. "Since we've wed," not "Since I've taken you in.") People seem to be taking their work north to Sepphoris, testing the craftsmanship of Abner. (Could his work be worth the trip?)

Joseph is concerned for his father's future, for ours. Last time he was down in Bethlehem, his uncle Samuel said there was enough work to keep another man busy. People moving out from the city. He'd take Joseph on like a son.

He wants to get down and settled before winter. Maybe when he goes down to Jerusalem for the feast after the harvest.

Great . . . Fine . . .

I don't know a soul in Bethlehem. They're his relatives, strangers to me—Ruth walking in from Moab. At the mercy of a whole clan of in-laws, aunts, uncles, cousins.

I asked him for time. A few more months here to drink in the courage of the Galilean hills. So I can face the good-byes. So I can comfort Mother. So the wrenching is eased.

He didn't give me a straight answer. Said I'd better feast my eyes and drink all I can hold. "And you'll be surprised. Judea offers a courage of its own."

There was the concern of Zechariah that this child be born in Judea. Maybe this is the Lord's push and provision.

"Couldn't we go down for just a few months and then come back? After the birth and dedication? Joseph don't you think? People will forget? You'll be needed here?"

"I'm thinking, Mary. I'm thinking."

He's thinking. What's he thinking?

He's thinking we should let this house go and take with us what we need to settle in Bethlehem. We don't have to make firm decisions about how long we'll stay. We don't have to tell Mother we'll never be back to live. It could depend on his workload. His relationship with Samuel. Word from his father back here. Herod's madness.

I think it could also depend on the measure of my content, though neither of us is likely ever to say it. ·

Mother and Dad for dinner tomorrow night. I told Joseph he mustn't broach the subject of moving until after the meal. Otherwise Mother won't eat. I'll serve lentil stew, which I've perfected somewhat. Start it early. Hold the rosemary. Dare I hope to turn out a dish Esau would sell his birthright for?

First the good news: Mother said the stew "hit the spot," which is, I guess, a compliment. The men said nothing, though the pot was bread-scraped clean, which is, I guess, a compliment.

The bad news: Mother fell apart. Wouldn't hear of Joseph's proposal, as if the great sea would be separating her from me, as if I were the last cord tying her to life.

Hadn't Zechariah taken away her favorite and oldest sister? Hadn't Zebedee stolen away our dear Salome? (Does my own sister off in Capernaum even know that my wedding celebration has been, well, say it, canceled? That I'm living as Joseph's wife?)

Her grief and anger were so out of character. Will He who made me like milk now curdle me like cheese?

Why had she bolstered my faith for such an impossibility when now . . . Maybe it's this: She stood firm and believed against all odds when her hope was for blessing. In this move away, she can see no gift, only theft. Joseph the thief. Giving me—us—a semblance of honor (forgive me, I should be more generous, considering my fated options), then turning around and taking me away, and her grandson. Think of it: The child of promise, to be born at the knees of a stranger, not his own grandmother who is far from the grave and spry enough to deliver triplets with her own hand.

Mother, he is my husband, and a kind one. I must be with him. It's the decision you would make for yourself. Why is it so hard to wish the same for a daughter?

The Lord gives. The Lord takes away. Blessed be the name of the Lord.

Mother has come down with a fever that has me frightened. She sees and swats cobwebs that aren't there. Or she wrings her hands as if she were washing them, asking for a towel. Her eyes focus in on my face. She calls me her little Mary and calls out for me to find a towel and wipe the dirt off my face.

With one hand I wipe the sweat from her forehead.

(If it weren't for the fever I'd think she was mimicking David feigning madness.) With the other I try to hold down her hands, maybe in comfort, maybe just to give me a sense of control.

I sing to her—Psalm 51: Lord, cleanse me with hyssop, and I will be clean; wash me, and I will be whiter than snow.

Am I easing her burden or only compounding her obsession?

It is impossible to tend two households at the same time. Joseph comes here to eat but goes home to sleep. Last night I stayed with Mother and Dad.

Dad says Mother is being punished for her outspoken opposition to Joseph's plan. He says we must go.

The first time ever—Joseph was sharp with me, this evening, just before Mother's fever broke. Called me into the yard, telling me I had to come home tonight. I would be sick with the fever if I did not sleep myself. Leave the tending to Father or call in Cousin Leah.

Joseph says a big job came in. We will stay till it is finished and then see.

The gall—this child punched out my navel, that wine goblet of beauty. Gone. Shattered.

Whose body is this anyway?

A good harvest year and so much to be thankful for.

Joseph gone to Jerusalem for the Feast of Booths and I at Mother's for the duration. So fortunate that Joseph's mother and family go down to visit their Bethlehem relatives. Otherwise I should have to stay under her roof.

I think Mother would have gone to visit Elizabeth had she not wanted an excuse for me to come home. She's delighted to have me here, to fuss over.

Wife of Rebekah's brother has died birthing her third child, a very small girl whose face is purple down one side, cheekbone to collarbone. Rebekah's mother is scurrying to save her. Heart-broken, imagining what sin might have caused this stain. With enough oil and balsam the spot might wash out. The child's father should return home tonight to such news.

As should Joseph and Father . . .

I had to ask for the few details I got, but Joseph talked to his uncle Samuel who still encourages him to move south. Lord, make our paths straight.

Rebekah's brother wants nothing to do with the baby. Will not look at her. Claims it cannot be his. Yet Rebekah's mother shuttles the girl among women who can spare milk, defying him and death itself.

The day I would have married. Mother remembered, and Joseph's mother came by today, bringing over a needle and spool of thread I left there, which she could have easily sent home this evening with Joseph. "You know what a lavish feast we were going to put out. Such a good harvest year. And isn't it one of the most lovely days of the year . . ."

"Yes, Mother Judith. It is."

I just can't imagine that Joseph could forget, yet he didn't mention it. (Nor did I.) Maybe he thought that I had forgotten—otherwise I would have made reference . . . Maybe he knew I wouldn't forget but figured I just wouldn't want to talk about it.

Maybe . . . is it possible that he just plain forgot?

The Psalm: Even the darkness is not dark to our God.

A womb. Is there a darker place? Month upon month of night.

What do you say? Maybe there's a reason for the full moon's power on the plug—as a call to the light while it may be found.

So will this boychild come when the moon is full? I just asked Joseph who gives no answer, as if it's a silly, woman's question. Tomorrow I will ask Mother, who will smile and say she wagers yes.

Jonah in the Fish

I've crouched here before in the dark
puzzling my break
through ribbed roofs and fatty walls.
I'm no Samson, bare hands
blessed to tear out life.
No David, practiced
and armed with stones.
I'm a boy unborn, wary but willing
to kick loose the bonds of flesh.

*Wretched Jonah, begging Heaven
for a whoosh and clean air.*

The early rains are pelting, blown by the breath of
God, always angry this time of year. Yet if His breath
were not as fierce, would the rain be forced to fall?
And if drought, then starvation. And so we are
blessed each year before and after winter. Blessed
with the anger of God.

Soldiers came riding through today, shutting the
shops, calling the tillers in from the fields—to hear a
decree. A census. Everyone must register his depen-
dents in the town of his birth and during the month
that starts next week. The month of my delivery.
Bethlehem.

Much of the town is angry. Joseph is somewhat
resigned. He says it's a sign. If he is forced by these
heathens to travel to Bethlehem—when there is no
holy day, when he has no urgent trade, when the winter chill is lord of the night, when his work here is
again tenuous—then we will let this house go and
leave with the intention of settling in Bethlehem.

His word was gentle but firm; he did not want my
opinion. We will stay with his uncle until we can find
a place of our own. We will go next week and take all
we can, for sure his tools, loading his donkey Sal.
(Aside: He felt he had to offer to pay his father for the
tools he's always used and now would like to take.
Father Jacob said no. Gave them with his blessing.)
When Father Jacob and Joseph's older brother come
later in the month to register their own families, they

will bring the rest of our goods. "It couldn't have worked out better, Mary."

I gave one opinion: If we load up Sal, if I must walk the length of the land carrying this child-weight (and the weight of Mother's good-bye, though I did not say it), the pace must be slow—over five days instead of three, staying one night with Elizabeth.

"Yes, as you say."

Mostly I don't think of it, but this morning I did look at the town with eyes that wonder if I will ever again live here. Am I destined to be a Judean? (Even though I live there and am married to one, is it possible for me to shed this Galilean skin—become "cultured"?)

As I said, mostly I don't think of it. (Am I burying my head under the blankets, turning my face to the wall?)

Think of yourself as Isaac's Rebekah, leaving home for a strange—and better—land. Adventure. Just go. Be grateful you're heading for the city of David and not some God-forsaken heathen land, like Egypt.

When Father saw that tonight was the night of the new-month fires, he ran over here so Joseph and I would come out to the cliff with him and Mother. I went with them. Joseph came in a few minutes, having gone by his father's home to fetch little Mary, hoisted onto his shoulders. Her excitement was contagious. I was four years old again, running my fingers through my father's beard and thinking him the wisest if not handsomest man alive.

Father was chatty and philosophical. No, he did

not regret having taught me what he could—as if I were the son who never caught his breath and died in Dad's arms the very day of his circumcision. He liked to believe that my knowledge of the Scriptures had turned my heart toward Heaven and Heaven's favor toward me. And Joseph, a finer son-in-law couldn't be found in Israel.

Mother was sullen, clinging to my arm as if she were a widow twice her age. (That fever did add ten years to and steal ten pounds from her frame.)

Before leaving, Dad prayed a blessing on new beginnings. The month ahead. Our journey. He blessed his house and ours.

We will leave right after the Sabbath, in two days. Though this wasn't our final good-bye, it was our first and possibly most significant.

Only Joseph shed no tears.

I cannot bring myself to write of the final good-byes.

On the road two days. Eating bread this evening: "Mary, would that I could carry the child's weight in my body."

The offer touched me. So genuine and innocent.

Dread the dark, which brings the cold, though we have found shelter each night. There is a cold that shuts down the natural will to live. You have to force yourself to fight the winter night.

They say there are people who live amid snow that doesn't melt even under the high sun. They walk in it—or on it. Heave it like straw. Tunnel it like dirt. Melt it by fire—to wash.

I thank Glory He set His people down—and brought us back to—here, not there.

As it is, in this cold I sleep little and think of nothing but wanting to huddle in on top of myself. We—at least I—nap when we stop for rest throughout the day.

To let me rest, Joseph has more time on his hands than he's used to. Yesterday he went off scrounging down the riverbank and came back with a block of dry driftwood he says is destined to be whittled into a child's play-ball, about the width of a palm. He whittles and whistles and waits. And lets me sleep—his rolled, dusty cloak as my pillow.

Went to the river. Bathed and sat to soak my fat feet. One day might Heaven grant that they be beautiful again?

Elizabeth's embrace, as warm as a mother's. And the look Zechariah gave Joseph: a father's pride, almost reverential.

A late night of laughter, and they have compelled us to stay several days, continue on after the Sabbath rest and feast.

Their John is a headstrong handful. One grace calls for another. He's a chubby little thing, still licking honey from his mother's finger.

Elizabeth has pulled out jars of oils and balms that I never saw while I was here with her. She must have oiled her own old skin in her private bath. But now she hovers and fusses over me and my stretched flesh as if I were the babe in her arms. There is a comfort in her care.

"This trip has been hard. You will deliver soon," she says, laughs. "The next full moon, you see . . ."

Good-bye to Elizabeth with great assurances that she will see this child soon—when I come to the city for my purification.

Her blessing: May He who delivered Daniel from the power of the lions, deliver you in your hour of distress.

Amen.

PART 4

Deliverances

Writhe in agony, O Daughter of Zion,
like a woman in labor, for now you must
leave the city to camp in the open field.
You will go to Babylon; there you will be
rescued. There the Lord will redeem you
out of the hand of your enemies

—*Micah*

Arrived safely—to what might be chaos but is pretty well under control.

Yes, yes, Uncle Samuel is delighted to see us.

Yes, yes, welcome kinsmen, welcome.

But this census has brought the wandering family home, and there's more to follow. Joseph's great uncle—and wife—arrived before the Sabbath. He intended to register today and leave, but his wife, Aunt Sarah, has taken ill, for two days in a deep sleep and now unable to move her right arm and leg or talk, though they can force her to swallow.

At least the house has a guest room—where she lies, Uncle Hilkiah night and day at her side and others in and out.

That means the rest of us—Uncle Samuel, Aunt Milcah, their Ophrah (with a stubbed hand) and Basemath (betrothed to marry next autumn, scratchy unpleasant voice), and Joseph and I—share the cozy family room. That's for now. As I said, they expect that more—seven more uncles or brothers or nephews (and wives?)—will show up between now and the end of the month. A census. One way to get to know the family.

I like Aunt Milcah. Her welcome is genuine and she takes the disorder in stride. Joseph says she's used to everyone coming in for the pilgrimage feasts.

The village is angry with Caesar, angry with Herod. Just angry. God's people should not be writing their names in the registers of foreign emperors.

But Joseph will. In the morning.

Tonight he set his jaw: "I will do this but the boy will not."

Joseph says his father is a better carpenter than his uncle, more exacting. What an irony—that Samuel the Sloppy has more work than he can handle and yet Jacob the Just-So is the one whose work has slacked off, though the reasons are obvious enough. (And maybe my reasoning is all wrong: It's not that Jacob's work slacked off, but that Joseph's did.)

Here, outside the family walls (the family does know of the altered autumn wedding plans), we have no story that raises eyebrows. People smile: a young couple, bless them, soon expecting their first (may it be) son of Israel.

Thank you. And yes, I feel certain it is a boy. And may it be soon, very soon. He weighs so heavy and low.

I have quickly found a friend in Joseph's cousin Rachel who lives a street over and is nursing a boy-child Benjamin, ten months old. A girl (how can I call anyone younger than I a woman?) of laughter and praise and thought.

I'd prefer spending the days at her house but am needed here. More relatives have arrived, though they won't stay long. And Rachel now has a houseful herself, of husband's kin.

Thinking today of Hannah, mother of Samuel, desperate in her desire for a child and radiant in the gift finally given her. But the story is more complicated with her being Elkanah's second wife. (Well, maybe his first, but what difference does order make when "she" has children and you don't?)

It is hard enough sharing a house with any woman but your own mother and maybe sister. What if I were asked also to share the attentions of my husband?

It *is* asked of some. May the burden stay far from my door.

We're getting close to a full moon. Maybe two more days. Aunt Sarah does not improve. They talk now of ways they can manage to get her home, maybe next week, several men carrying her on a cot Joseph says he will make.

There is no housing available to rent right now. Uncle Samuel makes it clear to his customers that we are looking for a place. Nothing. Nothing. Though how would we manage on our own when Father Jacob has not arrived with our housegoods?

Aunt Milcah called in the midwife, who says she will expect to return tomorrow, at the full moon, though she has another as heavy as I and doesn't know how she'll be at two places at the same time.

She is a little gruff. Aunt Milcah says she's very skilled, prides herself in coaxing out babies and their breath—while prodding women to hold on to theirs. "That's what counts so don't you fret yourself that she doesn't smile enough. You hear?"

Yes, I heard. Yes, that's what counts, but I started to cry a little anyway. For wishing to be home with Mother. For fear of this body ripping open, out of my control. For fear of I don't know exactly what. The terrors that sometimes seem ubiquitous.

I sang the brave songs to Elizabeth; who will sing them for me?

Some guests have gone, more have come. I can hardly keep track of the aunts and uncles—who is married to whom? This is a family blessed with numbers.

There aren't sleeping mats to go around, though Aunt Milcah won't hear of our going without. Would I disgrace her as a hostess by refusing the best she can offer?

No. No. So we two share a mat in a corner, against the far wall, and she sleeps on the floor, her big backside nearly falling in one of the mangers.

Would she disgrace herself as a hostess by offering the guest room to any but those who have been here the longest?

No. No. So if my time comes before Aunt Sarah and Uncle leave, I will deliver out here in the big room—as if I were a member of the family, not a pampered guest. As it should be, I guess.

Later: Rachel says she will come over and sing me the songs.

My pain started as we were serving up dinner. (The full moon hardly in the sky!) Aunt Milcah let the men eat and then shooed them out, to Rachel's for the night, though Ophrah and Joseph by way of the midwife's. Milcah says the father should always be sent to get the midwife—a temporary distraction.

As he left, Joseph whispered blessings. As he walked out the door, he turned back, his eyes betraying fear—and hope.

May his prayers relieve me through this night. And why shouldn't I expect that a miracle head off this pain, open the gates with ease?

But aren't we both sure that he will sleep tonight in Rachel's house more than I, here beside this manger, pacing, squatting, pushing, pleading?

I was spared no pain, but it seemed of little consequence once the breath filled his lungs.

And then near dawn shepherds at the door, visited by heavenly beings, one, then a skyful, announcing our news: the Anointed One, born, wrapped and in a manger. Rejoice. Praise the Most High.

Heavenly messages to Elizabeth, Zechariah, Joseph, and now seven shepherds, strangers, and a dirty, unkempt breed. Why would the Lord send such a grand word to such an earthy bunch? From what I can figure, no one in the town saw or heard the choir, which, to hear the shepherds tell it, would have been hard for anyone awake to miss. Joseph says it would have been just as he was on his way home, just as the midwife was rushing off (everything tied up here) to her second delivery.

As tired as I was, I wanted to hear every detail of their story, which they would have told me anyway, even if I'd fallen asleep before the end. One of them, I think his name was Jered, was young, barely a man, and he could hardly contain himself. You'd have thought he'd never seen a baby before, though it was the angels who had mesmerized him—their sudden appearance, their message, their praises, their departure, the sky suddenly as dark as any other cloudless night.

He asked if I'd already known that this was the Holy Child, or if they were the first and only to have been told. I said an angel—one angel—had told me and also Joseph. But a whole choir?

More later. Must sleep, though how in this mayhem?

Rachel was here, holding my hands. I fear I squeezed them flat as bread (and bit into a knotted clean rag). I was trying hard not to let my nails dig in to her palms.

I am torn and sore and tired. And the fuss—the family would be enough but the whole town is in and out, gawking, cooing, exclaiming.

It all makes me want to pick him up and run away (if I had the strength), maybe back to Nazareth, maybe to Elizabeth's arms . . . to some place where I would feel secure in him being my baby and not a child who belongs to every jealous Jewish mother who knocks on the door asking to see him. (Forgive me! I didn't mean to . . .)

Of course I don't run away. Instead I cry at the least provocation. But why when any other woman would be overwhelmed with positive emotion?

He's beautiful. Perfectly knit, top to little round bottom to tiny pink toes—all ten of them. I unwrap him too often just to look at him, to check once more and see if he's all boy. But each time he's the same, as fleshy as I, as male as Joseph, as predictable as any baby born to any woman on any night. Crying in wails. Leaking water. Sucking my breast. Burping his gas. He sleeps and sleeps and who knows what he dreams?

In my dream last night I heard the song the angels sang to the shepherds. I woke feeling as if the dream had been a gift, a reward for my labors, as if this squirming bundle weren't enough.

This morning down on the lower level, on his way toward the door and the shop, Joseph stopped to peer over Jesus, set in the day's fresh manger straw. Not very aware of my presence—or anybody's—Joseph talked to the baby as if he were an adult: "Hello there, and welcome to this fine house, a little crowded right now but we'll find a place of our own soon enough, don't you worry. My name is Joseph ben Jacob but you can call me Dad. . . ."

I'm quite sure he's smaller than Elizabeth's John was. He is so fragile, no, not fragile, vulnerable. I suppose it's true with every baby, but do you notice until it's your own? He can't even roll over. Can't find my breast; I have to find him to feed him.

That youngest shepherd came by today. Seemed out of breath, nervous, and in a hurry to leave. I think he didn't have permission to be away. "He's the Holy One," he said, as if I might have forgotten and it was his job to remind me.

Father Jacob arrived last night with our housegoods. He is obviously proud to have a new grandson and one so acclaimed, though he's puzzled, even skeptical, that a child conceived in impatient passion (if he only knew) could be so blessed. (He didn't see the band of shepherds. And what you hear third-hand you sift with reason.)

I don't know if Joseph has told him that he had an angel-dream message that this was a special child. And as for me—Father Jacob would never think to ask.

Jacob smiles at Jesus, hovers over him—but won't pick him up. Seems afraid he might do him harm. Joseph doesn't remember him picking up any of his grandchildren as infants, or even little Mary.

He intended to stay over the Sabbath and leave on the first day. Joseph tries to persuade him to stay longer, for the circumcision. But it's arranged that on their way north he and Joseph's brother will accompany Uncle Hilkiah, carrying Aunt Sarah home to Lydda. So Jacob says he'll already be getting back to Nazareth so late that Joseph's mother will be pacing like a penned lion. (These men—they claim to be rulers of their homes, but for love or fear they are ruled.)

Have no more to say here as I must write a letter to send back to Mother. With written words alone I can't begin to close the gap between us—dug by distance. As futile as it seems, I must try. Let her imagination, experience, and knowledge of me fill in the details—I would hope not too askew.

Jacob left us with a blessing and two shekels of silver, nearly half of the five shekels required to redeem a firstborn son. I didn't see the exchange, so I don't know what transpired but I'm surprised that Joseph accepted the money.

Joseph sobered this evening. Says he is more keenly aware now—than when we left Nazareth—that he may never again work at his father's bench.

Tonight we move to the guest room, Jesus taking his place sleeping between us.

His flesh must be cut. There is no other way. I must stand back and let the *mohel* (as experienced in his work as the midwife is in hers) pierce his flesh and prod his wails. For the glory of the Most High. As a sign of the covenant cut with His people. As a sign that this boychild has been purified, clean.

But I can't think of a knife being raised. There's no comparison of course (it's the harmless altering of his member), but the act reminds me of Father Abraham on Moriah standing over altared Isaac. And then of Mother Sarah. The rabbis tell her story, wound around her son's:

From the mountain Isaac, a grown, bearded man, did not return directly home with Abraham. When Sarah—watching for their return—saw Abraham approach without Isaac at his side, her life left, her heart stopped at the thought of Isaac dead as a bled animal.

Must stop this reflection, which weighs down my own heart, blocking the joy of the celebration: the mark of the Lord's people.

The eighth day. Circumcision. I have never seen Joseph as happy as he was today. Celebrating as I always imagined he would at his—our—wedding.

At the celebration Joseph repeated the words of his dream messenger, though without attribution: His name is Jesus—the one who saves—for he shall save his people from their sins. I waited half a year for one deliverance and now must wait a generation for another, which I can't imagine clearly in my mind. Can any mother picture her crying baby grown, commanding authority, moving empires and saving kingdoms?

I can hardly speak my boy's name without thinking of the promised salvation he will bring our people. And yet here he is, eleven days old, helpless and squalling in discomfort beyond his control or mine.

An old man (not crazy like Nathan) a few houses from Rachel's has died and Joseph has inquired about renting his house.

Yes, it is ours. Next week.

I woke this morning from a dream: washing rags, though at home and with singing Mother. What makes the duties of a day echo loud through a night?

Jesus slept through last night. Joseph says he must have known it was the Sabbath rest.

Rachel: "I know your Jesus is destined to save our people, so I've been praying that my Benjamin will be at his side when he enters Jerusalem."

I just stared at her and couldn't find words. My first reaction was "she's jealous," probably because it's the kind of thing Judith back home would have said with tainted motives. But then I decided her comment was innocent. She wanted the best possible future for her son, and for him she was dreaming that he'd been born for such a time as this.

When I stood there speechless we both got misty-eyed, overcome with emotion that was mostly positive: hope, I'd say, for what the Lord will work through our children.

But maybe it was also a little negative: A brief silent sorrow that only one of us had been chosen to bear the Savior of our people, only one of our sons would deliver his generation.

There are singular blessings—if given to one they cannot be given to another. I was glad to catch the moment in which I could glimpse and share Rachel's grief.

In the end I did say something: "I don't know why I was chosen . . . Yes, may Benjamin be at my son's right hand."

That's what I said, though now, looking back, I wonder where Zechariah's John will fit in.

This idea of being chosen: If I had grown up in another town, Bethlehem instead of Nazareth, Rachel instead of Judith would have been my childhood friend. (Such a small town doesn't have all that many girls of an age.) The basics of environment are chosen for a child. Even my child?

The harbinger of spring: the pink almond blossoms are popping open.

In two days we go to the city. My purification. My boychild's redemption. From there Joseph agrees we can go on for an overnight with Zechariah and Elizabeth. Then when we come back the house will be ready.

I am more than ready to be cleansed of this filth of the flesh.

I've gone back and read several of my recent entries. I've been referring to Jesus as *mine*—my boy, my baby, my Jesus. I wonder if I have any right to the possession those words imply—mine, my.

Sanctified or insane? I can't discern, as I have in previous times. Today, yet another word (unsettling, this one) again to—or from—strangers, the holy ones in the temple who pray night and day and wait for the rustling of holy winds. They, well, the old man, spoke of Gentiles (my son to have dealings with pagans?), of falling—and rising—of our own people, of piercing swords. Here:

In the temple court a tippy Simeon hailed us down. Wielding a cane so we would stop. Walking so slow he never would have caught up with us. An otherworldly look in his eyes.

At first cryptically he said he knew who this child was. The Most High had told him he would not die until he had seen this one: "May I be so honored as to take him in my arms?

"Now I may die in peace for I have seen the Lord's

salvation—come in this form that can be seen by all. A light for revelation to the Gentiles. The glory of Israel."

He blessed us and then continued with what sounded more like a curse: "The child, he will be spoken against. He will cause others to fall—and rise. And you," (he looked straight at me as an honorable stranger never looks at a woman's face; he felt excused by his age?), "his mother, a sword will pierce your own soul, too." The sharp word was spoken with warmth that left both Joseph and me bewildered, unsettled.

The messages of glory suddenly seem tainted by ominous clouds. What did this codger mean? Why did he add a "too" onto the end of his address to me? Was this just a crazy old man? (Maybe, but how can one know? Remember that Father made such claims of Zechariah when Dad could not reason through the message Z. sent.)

And then the old bent woman who joined our circle unbidden: She added her blessing and started creating a scene (help!), hailing like a beggar every passerby to call attention to her discovery. Did her presence contribute to the insanity or the sacredness of the situation?

Now, after this, I wonder about everyone I meet: Will this person—or that—realize I hold a holy child? Will this person—or that—burst into ecstatic praise at the sight of the most ordinary-looking bundle of swaddled flesh? Will this person—or that—pull me unwittingly into the center of a gazing crowd?

Elizabeth has such a way of calming my spirits and making me feel queenly. It's just something in the way she holds herself and approaches me. A second mother in a way Joseph's mother—or aunt—will never be.

She and Zechariah listened to our story of Simeon and Anna—also the shepherds. Did not understand Simeon's message but felt we should not discount it.

Figuring he'd have a little time on his hands, Joseph brought along the ball he's been whittling off and on since coming south. I had just assumed this was for our Jesus. Maybe it was intended so, but this afternoon Joseph deemed it finished and rolled it into baby John's reach. He is like a little emperor, claiming rights over occupied land.

We will leave the ball, and I hope Joseph finds another suitable "destined" block.

Home by noon and then moved right into the new house. I need my rest.

Joseph, mumbling and looking at my feet, says that the season of singing has come. Tonight. If I would be ready. It is good for him to state his intentions, give me the notice, though I have anticipated this coming once I was cleansed.

Now Adam knew Eve . . .

Why should I be like a veiled woman? . . . I am ready. He is no longer the stranger but the familiar love I'm ready to know and enfold.

(A thought: What if this marriage had started on a normal course? What if Joseph had not felt compelled to wait but had barged in with the vigor of youth? It would have been a different knowledge, the knowledge of the young, strangers groping at strangers. We are both older now—multiply the months of our marriage by years.)

I am ready, yet still nervous. Will I please him? Will he expect more than I know to give? I will gather rockrose gum before dinner and perfume my breastbone, bathed and oiled like a bride's.

Will his manhood disappoint me, having known the glory of the Lord?

As the night draws nigh I grow restless. It isn't fear, exactly.

Strengthen me with raisins, revive me with apples, for I am faint with love.

He is enough. A gazelle on the rugged hills.

Yesterday afternoon I may have talked of older love, but now the night seems to have been the frolic of children, fragile though oblivious to anything but the immediate thrill of their grip on life.

My lover is mine and I am his. Let him browse among the lilies.

A squared piece of wood has captured Joseph's fancy and by the light of the evening lamp he's taken to whittling Jesus a ball, about the width of my palm.

I had a wonderful day with Rachel—dying wool. Her Benjamin took his first step this morning: I reached down to pick him up and he lurched away from me and toward his mother. We kept laughing about it, about his willful determination to get out of my reach, as if I were a lion waiting to grab him.

Wouldn't it be nice if my Jesus' first steps were toward my open arms, as Benjamin's were toward Rachel's?

Benjamin. To him his mother is a fortress that is utterly trustworthy and secure. She is his food, his comfort in pain, his enfolding shelter from threatening strangers and storms.

Of course I see the same dependence (on me) in Jesus, but he is too young to reach for help and specifically from me as distinguishable from any other.

Too soon our babies will be schoolboys learning the limits of a mother's abilities. May they look to Heaven for their protection.

Do I love this child more than I love my Lord—as one might love a gift more than the giver?

He is jealous; He said so Himself, to Moses, on the mountain. It seems He was speaking of graven images but does He wince when a little one steals away a mother's heart? If so, am I excepted?

Be gracious Lord, to me, Your servant.

This husband: his actions and eyes speak of love for me, his body jumps at the thought of being one with me, his troth is pledged till death to me. And yet . . .

This husband: Once a day he prays and thanks the

Most High that he is not me, a woman born of a woman born of a woman.

He feels more blessed than I. And yet how could it be possible for someone to feel more blessed than I feel? Visited by an angel, who trusted me—alone— with his message. Bearer of this unnatural but natural child.

I pray that my blessing won't sour into pride. And yet I stake my claim—that I am blessed.

The whole town is out tonight, to see a new eastern star that overshadows all the others. Quite a stir about it last night and today. What does it say of the summer that follows this blooming spring?

My dear Mary,

You were out shopping this morning. I saw your book, which you always try to hide but never very well. Many days before I've been tempted to open it and read the thoughts you write but do not speak to me.

And today I opened it; it fell to this page first—where you stopped writing—and my conscience burned. I mustn't read.

I didn't read. But to assure both you and myself that I won't read the secrets of your heart on some future day when I ache to know, I write this pledge. I won't open your book again.

So, this being the only time I write to you in these pages, I tell you now that I am the most blessed man on earth to have you as my wife.

Write on.

Joseph

Gold. Frankincense. Myrrh.

Herod (such a heathen) wants to know where we live (such a humble house, whitewash worn off and walkstones askew).

Three star-struck visitors: wise Gentiles riding rich-man camels, wearing smooth-woven robes and kingly furs, yet bowing like shepherds to the floor, worshiping (dare I say it?) this boy on my knee.

What did I do? Cry. The surprise, the gifts, the Gentiles in my house (and yet hospitality and their incredible story demanded it), the mystery of the star (are the heavens being rearranged on account of this child?). The shame for our hut, our meager furnishings, our solitary, lowly ass. (Not that I'd seen them as so disgraceful in the past.)

The star, they said (one of their slaves knew our language well enough), was sure sign of a king's birth, no ordinary king—one they could not chance to miss. So they set out, followed it west, across desert and mountain to Judea and here. And last night it fell and burned out as it was about to hit this roof (so they said, though no one in town—and half the town was crowded around the door here—confirmed this last report). Signs. Signs.

Figuring they'd find a future king in a palace nursery, they stopped and asked questions in Jerusalem, talking even to Herod, who took an interest and sent them here, asking for a report so he can come also. (No. No. Keep that swine away.)

You'd think that with each surprise I'd be better prepared to handle the next, but that doesn't seem the case. With each surprise I feel more on edge, wondering what I will be confronted with next. What characters will appear, when, where, how, and with what news?

You expect a rather predictable Galilean, small-town life, and instead you see the stars moving—can it be?—on your account, well on your son's account but when he is still on your breast can you really separate yourself from your child?

Abraham welcomed three strangers: heavenly beings in earthly disguise. Not like my angel visitor who came and went in a moment—but eating and drinking with him, walking with him toward Sodom where they lodged with Lot. Heavenly beings in earthly disguise.

Who are these three, who came knocking on our door and are now lodging at the inn?

Joseph says we can't bury the gifts in the yard, as we might, because of the crowd of witnesses to their presentation. As I write by the light of the lamp, he's at my feet digging, burying them here in the floor of the house. The only safe place.

Oh yes, tonight the star seems to have disappeared or maybe melted back to its pinhole size.

The youngest of the visitors knocked on the door early this morning, even before dawn. Wanting to be as inconspicuous as possible, he was alone except for the one Hebrew slave.

Last night all three of the wise men had the same dream: Unbidden, a young man dressed in white had joined them for a meal. He'd said that they should not keep their word to Herod but quickly and quietly return home.

When the Gentile told us that the dream was a sign from God, Joseph glanced at me across the room. Weren't we both relieved at this news?

We wished him—them—God's peace, and as he turned to go he hesitantly asked if he could hold Jesus. Did he know what he was asking of us? A Gentile touching a Jewish baby, and one so destined?

I felt I must say yes: because he sees and understands wonders of our Lord; because he has sought the Lord from such a distance.

For just a moment he cradled Jesus on his forearm, with reverence yet an ease and a slight bounce that told me he has a young child back home.

So many people seem to know that he is a special child. Will our story one day be written and read like the story of Esther at Purim?

Oh, I can't think of it.

What next? In the middle of the night Joseph shook me awake and told me to get up, get dressed, and pack what we needed to travel; we had to leave for Egypt before dawn; he'd had a dream.

He was in no mood for questions—agitated yet very controlled and intent on his purposes, giving me orders. I'd never seen him like this and he frightened me.

By the time I got up he was dressed and gone—to rouse the donkey and kill our one pair of doves. He came back in to dig up the gifts, which I wrapped inside baby cloths and stuffed in baskets with figs and nuts and barley.

I asked if I could go over to Rachel's to give an explanation. No—though I saw that he left a cryptic note: Don't worry. We must go.

Just as we left I yanked two spring lilies from the yard and laid them between Jesus' breast and mine.

As we hurried out of town, I thought of Lot fleeing Sodom. He—or his wife—didn't even have time to pick lilies.

I don't know which is worse—traveling at a slow pace when you're heavy with a wombed child or at a clip when you're carrying a three-month-old, though I must admit that Joseph carried Jesus whenever he was asleep or content to be off my breast.

I ran on nerve—and grace—until we stopped near dusk to make camp. The roasting doves were just beginning to brown when I burst into tears. Joseph held me, which was fine, but both doves burned on one side.

Joseph had talked some throughout the day. The messenger—the same one who'd told him to take me as wife—had warned him of Herod's wildfire anger. The baby's in danger; there's no room for two Judean kings.

The "get out" was so urgent he feels we must drive just as hard tomorrow as today to get over the border.

(Can you believe this: being asked to flee the Land of Promise to find refuge in Pharaoh's land of slavery?)

Now that we've eaten I'm ready to walk till I drop if I have to—to save my boy. I'd even stand between him and the devil and fight—like a man.

I thought a lot today about this exile and the burden I lay at the feet of our stargazing visitors. If only they hadn't stopped in Jerusalem. If only they hadn't made such a fuss. Why did Herod have to get wind of the birth of a peasant king? (Oh how clearly I see the wisdom of Mother's original advice to keep my knowings to myself.)

They were surely holy men who listened for the Lord's voice. And if He told them not to return home by way of Jerusalem, why didn't He tell them to come straight to our house in Bethlehem and stay away from Herod in the first place?

Did the Lord speak and they not hear? Did the Lord mean for them to follow the star nonstop—straight through the capital? Could the Lord of the universe have meant for us to be driven from our home? Could He want such a boy to sing his first songs in a foreign land?

He's asleep here beside me. Will I ever grow tired of looking at his face? Of slipping my finger like a rod through his fat little fist? Of kissing his forehead?

He'll never remember this trip. It's just as well . . .

I wish I'd had time to say good-bye to Rachel.

I feel so sick I can't eat. The babies are dead. Oh, Rachel, why was Benjamin torn from your arms?

About noon we noticed several horsemen on the horizon behind us. Being safe, across the border, we slowed to let them catch up. They were from Jerusalem, and when Joseph mentioned that we'd come from Bethlehem they all stared at Jesus, then at me, and then at each other.

Something was amiss and Joseph asked.

"The village—House of Bread—has become the House of Death," one said. Two days after we'd left, a battalion of soldiers descended like a wolf pack.

Sneering "Death to the king," they broke down doors, searched caves and barns and fields and stabbed every boychild less than two years old. Every one. Dead.

Joseph's dream. What if we hadn't obeyed?

Jesus lies in front of me on his blanket giggling at his hands as if they were toys bought at the market.

I sit here under a scraggly pine tree silently crying, though I can't clearly identify the cause of my tears. They are joy and gratitude for his laughter. Relief after narrowly escaped disaster. Grief for my mourning sister. Horror at the thought of the innocents' slaughter.

Why my Lord?

Little Moses—by Heaven spared from Pharaoh's hand.

My Jesus—by Heaven spared from Herod's sword.

That question, What if we hadn't obeyed the messenger in Joseph's dream? haunts me. If we'd started to make travel plans but proceeded slowly, would Heaven have pricked at our thoughts with a thousand needles till we could no longer stand still but had to run away? If we'd stayed in town, would Heaven have sent an army of angels to keep the soldiers away from our door? Was there really a chance that Herod might have succeeded? How responsible are Joseph and I for this holy child's life?

And another thought keeps coming to my mind. Lot's wife. Did she have a friend like Rachel whom she'd left behind?

Last night's nightmare: I was walking, running, staggering, down our Bethlehem street, trying to escape. With my body I hovered over Jesus, trying to shelter him even though he was already dead. I put my hand to his forehead and it was cold but I kept running anyway, till I got out of town where I collapsed. I was sobbing and I unwrapped him, hoping maybe if I rubbed him I could bring back the warmth.

I hadn't actually seen anyone touch him and there was no blood until I got down to his skin. There was a huge open gash down the side of his baby-fat belly. I tried to shake him back to life and I woke up. Joseph was shaking me, asking me what was wrong.

Of course Jesus was fine. I reached for him and touched his face. I listened to his heavy breathing for a long time before I went back to sleep. But this morning when I changed him, I held my breath for a second just before I saw his bare stomach. Would it be as smooth and soft, flawless and warm, as it was yesterday? I ran my hand across it. I poked at him, walked a "spider" up his chin, blew at his navel until he laughed.

Not till that moment was my heart sure that he'd come back to life.

I'm just recovering from a cold that rendered me useless for several days, and at such a critical time. Cough lingers. Cannot write.

PART 5

Consolations

You will nurse and be carried on her
arm and dandled on her knees.
As a mother comforts her child,
so will I comfort you.

—*Isaiah*

Queries and crossroads have led us here to a Jewish settlement near the base of the Nile Delta. We sold the frankincense, with gratitude for the Lord's provision.

We found a house in one day. Joseph has inquired about the carpenters' guild, strong here. He has a day job tomorrow and is on edge. Here he has no family references to rely on. His craftsmanship must speak for itself. Such a tight guild—they even worship together in a certain section of the synagogue—means he and his work will be judged quickly. Though an outsider, may he be deemed gifted and chosen, like Bezalel and Oholiab, the craftsmen of Moses.

Rachel still on my mind. Does she hate me? Does she blame us directly, indirectly? Does she know—or even care—that we are safe?

Scenario 1—Rachel, angry and bitter in the manner of the mother whom Solomon judged a liar: If my son is dead, yours should be too . . . "If I had the courage I would run a spear through the baby-flesh of your boy—the one they were looking for, the one my Benjamin died for.

"Why did we welcome you here? Why didn't you stay in Galilee, out of my life—peaceful until your grand boasts stirred Herod to throw lightning that split me in two?

"It is good you are gone—to the hills or the desert

or the grave—or else I would tear at your face with my nails. If I must wail, why not you?"

Scenario 2—Rachel, consumed with grief but trying to walk in the way of understanding: "Mary, my tears are my words. I look for consolation and find little, except in your escape . . ."

Which?

I can only hope.

Thoughts of this slaughter bring back another memory: Old-man Simeon and his talk of swords piercing flesh—mine and . . . My Lord, what was he talking about?

Steady now.

If it is possible, the Passover takes on deeper meaning when celebrated in the bowels of Egypt, though the Pharaohs are long dead.

Aren't we—living here—like the sons of Jacob, seeking (and finding) refuge from calamity in the land of promise? But then what? For their sons the sweet turned bitter, the life turned to death. For a time, until Heaven saw fit to deliver, sparing the sons at the sight of the lamb's blood.

Like a crazed woman I sweep five times the floors and walls to rid this house of any leaven—the sin of our people. We will not be found wanting. Here, even more than if we were back home, the household of Joseph will be prepared for the sacred feast of flight.

The best part of the day is the hour of dawn, when we three lie in bed almost awake: Jesus feeding; I praying, maybe singing, in spirit; Joseph—I can't be sure what's in his mind, but he is aware of our presence and more contented than he is in the evenings, when he comes home so tired.

The unfinished whittled ball was left behind in Bethlehem. This evening Joseph brought home a third block of wood—destined, he says.

Dear Mother,

There is no foreseen way for me to get this letter to you, yet I write it in the chance that I meet someone who would be traveling back near Nazareth. I would be ready to send this.

I can write highlights only, may the Most High grant me the chance to tell you in person the signs and wonders . . .

We are in Egypt—safe but not feeling at home—with a group of our people settled on the Nile—such a river you can't imagine. We had to leave Herod—warned in a dream to flee Bethlehem (we had found a house and settled in comfortably) before—we've received word—his soldiers came to town to spear . . . the babies.

I wish you could see—meet—our healthy, laughing Jesus. He likes to hear himself scream—in fun—and reaches now for me and even Joseph, though not for strangers. (Give him a day or two and he would know that you were his grandma.)

Joseph's father would have told you about the shepherd visitors. Then several months later, wise, cameled Gentiles from the east followed a bright star (did you see it in Nazareth?) right to our door. They left gifts, thank the Holy Name, which have fed us. There is more amazement to tell. Mother, who would believe this story?

On most days Joseph has work—so far being an extra on various jobs. It takes some time here to be hired directly for your own work. With Jesus he is as good as I can imagine a father to be—tender, attentive. But when anything goes wrong (whenever Jesus cries), he gives me that helpless look: Do something. Make the noise stop.

The women here are hospitable enough but think me reserved. They don't see me as one of them. Many have grown up here and cannot yearn to be in our land in the way I do. Then I'm not free to tell them any details of our journey to this place.

I pray that I will be able to see you and Father very soon. If that is not to be, know that our times—your times—are in the hands of the Almighty.

With my love,
Mary

Found Sal the ass stiff and cold this morning. Hosea next door came over and helped Joseph drag him out to burial. We can live without one for a little while, but not having a beast makes me feel trapped here, as if there were no escape.

Now why would we need to escape?

Yes, you want to go home, but you are safe here, at least more safe than in the grip of Herod who claims rule of the Land you love.

I am a solitary tree planted by the rivers of water. Whether by Mother's constraint or the Lord's, I don't know. But I still feel I must not talk about the most important and most perplexing issue in my life (an issue I can't push out of my mind for long as it—he —demands my hourly attention). Where does that leave me? Separate. Isolated. Alone with Joseph the Steady but Silent. Walking in the counsel of the community women but never feeling one of them. Mary, the Known but Unknown.

He—Jesus—listens. I talk—about our family, our people, the way we do the things we do, the way our God has been faithful to His faithless children. About Abraham and Sarah, Isaac and Jacob, Hannah and Esther.

I talk. He listens—though he can fall asleep (or start railing) right at the climax of the story.

You wonder what he's thinking—if anything—and what he would say if he could speak. I'm hungry? I love you? Let's play? When will Dad be home? Sing me a song?

And what will his first word be? *Mom? Dad?*

And when will we celebrate his first *amen*?

Mother insists—I think she heard what she wanted

to hear—my first word was a demanding *more*, referring to her breast.

He's worked slowly but Joseph has finally finished
the whittled ball, adding ridges—little rivers—around
the middle. Before we give it to Jesus I want to add
my stamp, staining the ridges mulberry purple.

Maybe the earth without form and void was like
bread dough that takes the shape of any bowl. Maybe
the Most High kneaded it in play, pushing it here and
there just for the pleasure of the palm.

No, can't be. Why would He ever have changed
the texture, pulling the wet out from the dry?

He seems to know the ball is his possession. If it has
his attention, he cries when he rolls it out of his
reach.

His days are lived at opposite poles—perpetual
motion or the stillness of sleep. Sleep, a small death,
they say. And with him it seems so, as when he's
"there" he doesn't hear the loudest, most irritating
noises—the children running by on their way home
from school, the new (young and still nervous) ass
fussing at traffic on the street . . .

How different from my sleep, so near the surface
of the deep. I hear every sputter he makes all night.

Hell—the place where one is forgotten, by family, friends, even God. Wiped from memory. The past months have been a taste of it, as the bitter herbs of Passover are a taste of our people's suffering in Egypt.

The Wisdom: "Do not say, 'Why were the old days better than these?'"

We invited Hosea and company to dinner to celebrate Jesus' first *amen*. It was half there—*men*, really, but there was no mistaking the tone and place of it, at the end of the dinner grace. A justifiable excuse for setting aside the afternoon weaving. Now that I've gotten the hang of it, I'd rather cook any time.

His first solitary, unsteady step, yes, toward me, though not away from a pursuer. He surprised himself, seemed happy for a second, then panicked that he had nothing to hold onto, until I rescued him. We danced around the room, singing praises and then a little chant: Wait until we tell Daddy.

We have been here nearly a year, and I still look for every thread that will tie me back to our land.

The cedar of Solomon's temple was carved with open flower blossoms. Since hearing that as a child I've always thought of the flowers of the field—the lilies, the rockroses, capers, mustard—as creations raising their perfumed hands and painted faces in praise to their Creator smiling down on them.

The flowers bloom here in the spring, as they did at home. I rejoice in their comfort and raise my hands with theirs.

Joseph, what would I do without him? When I feel as if I'm about to be pushed over the cliff, he always seems to step between me and the edge and he nudges me back to the safe ground. I think he'd say I do the same for him, though I never see it as such at the time.

The rabbi's sister has died, which means taking in food—stuffing the living who are consumed with the dying. Eat, eat. Tomorrow it mustn't be you.

To be so honored—such a gathering of women leading the bier. The whole city heard our wails.

A funeral procession—yet another reminder of our place as daughters of Eve: Since she brought death into the world, her daughters lead death's victims to the grave.

When I think about death, and Eve, I think of her facing it for the first time, weeping over the stiff body of her Abel—and then confronting her shamefaced Cain. Boys she bled for, suckled, laughed with. I can't imagine myself in the scene, and I was born into this sinful state; how much worse for her who had known an Eden where lambs had no reason to fear lions nor brothers—had there been brothers—each other. To know how far a generation had strayed—and to feel responsible for the cost. The mother in me weeps for the mother of us all.

With the heat we're sleeping on the roof these days. When Jesus wakes up I give him my breast, then tell him to listen to the morning. We look to the east to see the peeking sun and then to the fig tree to spy out the songbirds. He listens and looks and soon wakes up Joseph, ready for prayers.

He has two favorite songs: Moses' "the horse and rider He has hurled into the sea" and Noah's parade: "the lions, beetles, and bears lined up . . ." He chants, "Sing it again," and then laughs, as if it were a silly game.

A praise to Heaven for creating herbs and spices—the luxuries of taste and smell that make one pleased to linger over a table or simmering pot. A pinch of ground mustard seed, a sprig of rosemary, a bay leaf—like leaven in dough, such a small effort effects such great reward—or reform.

While I'm at it, why not mark my thanks for perfumes that wash the body-foul with fragrance?

Another Passover here. It is in capsule the entire history of our people—at the same time cause for sorrow and great rejoicing.

When we get back home (surely we *will* get back home), the very first new moon, I'm going to ask Father to take Jesus—well, all of us—out to the cliff to watch the new-month calendar fires that dot the bottom bowl of the night. Jesus is old enough to be enthralled with the scene. (I will be as excited as he.) And of course Father will pray a blessing on us pilgrims finally returned.

Jesus is taking the cup and eating porridge and bread—and biting my breasts till I yell and, today, bleed. That's enough. I've bound my ribs and he will get no more from me.

A foul day. Jesus woke begging my breast with such a fuss that Joseph growled for him to stop; he would have no more of this. Then Joseph was sour with me, as if this crying, then whimpering, were my fault, something I could have prevented, if I'd . . . who knows what.

I am so full and sore and this child is so cranky, I'm tempted to give in—as if I could delude myself and imagine that I could jump back in time to when he would suckle in quiet toothless gratitude.

I'm dry. Unbound. Cause for inviting friends for a feast. They say it's reason to celebrate, though today it feels reason to mourn the loss of that last physical tie to him. I was hardly aware of the midwife cutting the birthcord that bound him to me. But this cutting—I see it with wide-open eyes.

Joseph saw the angel again last night—in a dream. Herod is dead and we are to return home. But to

Joseph "home" refers to Bethlehem, not Nazareth as I would wish.

Tonight I will articulate my reasoning—aside from my desire to return to the family and Galilean hills that succored me in youth: If he thinks we will be outcasts in Nazareth, how much more so in Bethlehem, where people might well associate our strange story and midnight disappearance with Herod's swooping revenge. How can he expect us to walk into that town, settle in that town, and be one of them?

Yes, tonight I will lay out the argument for why our children should nestle in the arms of Galilee. Yes, I said "children." I have reason to think Joseph's seed has taken root in my womb. I will tell him that also.

It's a small comfort that he listens to me without interruption. There is some wisdom in his plans: We will head east as soon as reasonably possible (within the week; he will look for a caravan; we will sell our goods). One cannot reach Galilee except through Judea; once in Judea we will discern if it is well to settle there or to go north.

Why do I call his plans wise? They are cautious and measured in terms of our future. But more, they are cautious and measured in terms of our immediate household peace.

With his cavern eyes Joseph can say unspeakable words.

I challenged him on one more point: Could he be sure Herod is dead? Remember the history of our people: Jerusalem rumors once hailed the death of the

Syrian Antiochus Epiphanes—alive and, at news of his own demise, angered enough to plunder the city and kill eighty thousand. "Joseph, are you sure Herod is dead?"

He didn't answer me except with a stare. I'll attempt to translate: How dare you, who saw the angel of the Lord, question my sighting, my knowledge?

That's what he wanted me to hear, and I heard.

I do trust his discernment and his word, which has proven true in the past, and yet I am not at all sorry I asked the question.

And so we leave in the morning for home, wherever that proves to be.

Holy Name, please, Nazareth. The knot I carry in my stomach (alongside the sickening child) tightens at the thought of seeing Rachel. May I someday be ready for the reunion. But not now. Not yet.

I write this as I sit leaning against Joseph who is leaning against me. There is a comfort in this position—spine to spine. Maybe it reminds me of the first months of our marriage, before we slept face-to-face (though since then this little one has more than not snuggled between us).

Maybe it's a deeper symbol of being one. Two exhausted people, each propped up by the other. For this moment you can't determine who's giving and who's taking because they are one in the same.

Our stiff-necked people spent forty years crossing this desert, a journey we—slowed by the care of a child and by my wavering stomach—will complete in two weeks. I don't even know what forty years is, as I can't "see" the size of a canvas of time that is three times larger than the one I carry, going back to my first memories, safe in the clefts of Nazareth.

Yes, travelers coming from Jerusalem confirm that Herod is dead, his kingdom divided among three sons. Archelaus has established rule in Judea with a massacre—three thousand Jews dead.

There are no such reports from Galilee, ruled now by Herod Antipas.

Joseph weighs the message.

I claim it as one more reason to settle in Galilee.

To Nazareth, rugged Nazareth. I can smell the water running at the well. We'll travel quietly through Judea but up the coast, not near Bethlehem or Zechariah's to make our return known.

Father is dead and buried, less than a week. Found fallen over his potter's wheel, the wet clay crushed under his weight.

Sister Salome is here and ready to take Mother home with her to Capernaum. No, Mother must remain here with us—meaning we could settle here in her house and she stay on. All to be decided tomorrow.

Mother, Joseph's family—all overwhelmed at our appearing.

Mother overwhelmed, period. So intense that Jesus seems frightened of her—of all the commotion. Clings to me. Joseph left and took him out a long time, I guess to get acquainted with his little Mary, not so little anymore.

Salome somewhat hostile—in her grief, her total lack of understanding as to our marriage and absence . . . what she sees as our total lack of responsibility. "What has happened to you, Mary? You came of age and your head went soft."

Some warm welcome home to craggy Nazareth.

Mother to stay here with us, or we here with her. It is the arrangement she preferred.

Salome seemingly relieved with the plans. "Mary, you always were better with her." Translation: "Mary, you always were her favorite, so it only makes sense that you should have the patience to tend her."

So much comforting and mothering and managing to do that I haven't yet had time to tend my own grief. Having missed the funeral procession and burial, it's easy to think Father is off in Jerusalem at a feast. The commemorations make you face the realities.

Joseph buried the gold and myrrh in the back, under the fig.

Last night the moon was slivered and after dinner I insisted that we all walk out to the cliff to watch the new-month fires. Mother said she wouldn't come, though after we'd all left she yelled for me to wait up.

Joseph carried Jesus on his shoulders, and Jesus thought he was king of the world. He was excited to see the fires I must admit I'd been building up as a spectacular sight.

As we sat in the dark Joseph talked to Jesus—about the fires looking like stars, which reminded him of Jacob's young Joseph having a dream that the surrounding stars were bowing to his star, which made his brothers angry, from which we should learn not to share our dreams of grandeur, which reminded him of special visitors we'd had about the time he was born who followed an exceptionally bright star . . .

He went on and on but I paid little attention as Mother was sobbing her loss into my arms and I, mine into hers. In a while Jesus left Joseph, pushed his way between Mother and me, and also started crying.

Joseph left us alone for a few minutes but then said it was time to go. I didn't respond, and he started to pray a blessing over our new month, which only made Mother and me cry harder.

Well, we finally got everyone home and to bed, but it was one traumatic evening.

Deep in the night, when Mother was finally asleep, Joseph came to me, as if to offer comfort. As I was afraid she would, Mother woke up. By the time Joseph was snoring, Mother's breath was tellingly silent. Neither she nor I went back to sleep.

She is sullen today. We will all have to learn to adjust.

When I was four or five, in Jerusalem, Father stopped—he hardly ever stopped—at a vendor's booth. He put me on top of his shoulders and we pushed our way to the front of the crowd, where the man—young—was selling ice he'd galloped in from the mountain.

Father bought a piece, set me down on my feet, put it in my mouth, and told me it was candy to suck on, not chew. He took a piece for himself (did he buy one for Mother or Salome?) and started making funny faces at me—and I at him, to mimic him but also because I was so surprised at the cold. We laughed but before it was over I was crying, disappointed that it was tasteless, not sweet.

He felt bad, frustrated I suppose. His treat had turned sour.

Why has this come to my mind today?

Dear Father,

I am just beginning to understand that you are gone from us, not to return before the next Sabbath rest, before the next new moon, before the birth of your next grandchild who is now swelling my skirts.

I grieve for myself, for Mother, but also for my children; I wanted Jesus to sit on your knee, recite his lessons to you, see the contented joy evident on your face—knowing that another generation is hiding the Law deep in its heart. Even when I faced the possibility that we might raise our family in Bethlehem and not here in Nazareth, I envisioned your prayers of blessings that would tide me—us—over from one festive visit to the next.

I wish you could have seen our Jesus.

Do not worry for Mother. She is well with us.

Father, we will not forget you.

As you would wish, we will bless the Lord
from this time forth and forevermore.

Love Poem for Sleeping Joseph

Asleep, Jacob saw angels
climbing a ladder
stretched to heaven's floor,
where the Lord sat declaring blessings
on a lineage spread this far.
Awake, I lay my head
on your chest, softer
than Jacob's pillow,
and I listen to your rhythms
constant as the river flow.
When your breath goes under water
I wonder if you'll emerge
with another word from on high,
a slash through our routines:
Receive this child; take this woman;
flee this land. Now. Go.
I said. That's all. Good-bye.
Each time the lightning retreats
and leaves us in the dark:
You, me, and the boy,
a child of no dream
born to rule Jacob's ripened seed.

Sleep well tonight, my Joseph.
Wake with the sun, not before.
May angels guard our feet,
stand stone silent at our door.

Mother tells me that Cousin Leah has been bleeding for a year. Heaven does not answer her prayer, and why? Now the doctor has prescribed his cures. Three times he—or someone in his hire—was known to creep up behind her and bellow a noise that would scare the army of Gideon. But the river was not scared dry.

Mother says the doctor keeps watch over the great route east from Acco on the sea and the valley road, looking for a white mule—the sure carrier of her cure.

My prayers join with Leah's.

The wisdom of Jesus ben Sira: Sometimes healing is in the physicians' hands, since they ask for this grace that life may be saved.

My years in Egypt only heighten my sense of separation from the women here. They've traveled no farther than Jerusalem. It's hard for me to describe.

It's not that our devotion is affected by where we've been or what we've seen—or not seen.

It's just that they think of the Jordan as a big river. They think our summers are hot and our cities grand. They know the world is bigger than Galilee or Judea—the traders and soldiers are reminders—but they know it only in their heads; it's not real to them as it is to me—and to Joseph. I know he senses it too, though more of the men than the women have traveled.

It's one more thing that binds the two of us together.

Oh, Leah. I went over today and was greeted by one heartsick—and pale and thin—woman. Her Thomas, she says, is always sour. The children have caught the spirit that hangs over the whole house. Look at them and you can tell they're unhappy. As for the doctor—he found the white mule and told Leah to swallow the remedy: With no soothing-honey help, she dutifully ate the single (thank Heaven for small blessings) kernel of barley dug from the mule's dung. No relief.

She's tired. Says she has to rush through the day because she's always doing laundry. In the night she wakes up from dreams—of scrubbing stained rags.

It's easier for me to pray than for her. I'm new on the scene; I don't carry her day-in, day-out hope deferred. I don't live with a malcontent, blaming husband. I don't dream of cloths I can't wash clean.

I can pray—and I can carry water for her. Surely my shoulders can bear one more trip to the well each day. Will also shop for her in Sepphoris; we need to go up for ourselves anyway.

In the synagogue Joseph read the closing Sabbath Scripture, from the prophets, Isaiah's description of the branch of Jesse: "The Spirit of the Lord will rest upon him, the spirit of wisdom and understanding, the spirit of counsel and power, the spirit of knowledge and of the fear of the Lord. (The fear of the Lord is his breath.) He will not judge by what his eyes see or his ears hear. He will judge the poor with righteousness and justice."

At the end of his reading, before his reflection

(inspired to my ears, though nothing extraordinary if I accurately read the congregation's response), he glanced up to me, pressed at the front of the women's gallery. (Mother and I had gone to service early to stake a prime place.) If circumstances had permitted, his glance would have been a smile.

On several levels his reading seemed a symbolic welcoming back into the fold of the community.

Poem for Leah: The Woman's Issue

By day blood floods my dreams,
by night, frames them in dirty laundry.
If someone would shut my womb
tighter than Sarah's, I would rest,
relieved to be empty as Elijah's tomb
and clean as unused linen.

I wrote it and there it lies on paper, but I'm not sure I'll ever show it to her. Maybe later.

My domestic routines vary hardly a jot from Mother's, and yet . . . I see that I'm used to being in charge of them. Stopping for a breather at (my) will. Seasoning my own pot. Fanning my own fire. Singing the songs that light in my own mind.

Between my awareness of Leah's condition and my own bulging belly, I'm particularly aware of the blessings and curses of a woman's womb. Questions:

How is it both our glory and shame?

Why is our sex something men detest by

day—thanking Heaven they are not one of us—yet beg for by night, restless until we are one and they are withered?

Are men so desperate to return to the safety of their mother's womb?

And God. Does He have a womb? Why did He challenge Job: From whose womb comes the ice? Who gives birth to the frost? Does I AM know what we bear?

I pray for more understanding of this One who refers to Himself as both "us" and "me."

Tried to explain death to Jesus and think I did it badly. Had him put his fingers close to his open mouth and feel the warmth of his breath—the breath of God, life, I explained. Then I put his hand to my breath, and mine to his. I put his hand on his chest so he could feel the steady rise and fall—another part of breath.

The lesson: The Most High breathed His life into Adam's mouth—and yours and mine and Dad's and Grandmum's and all the people we see in the village. But someday the Lord decides that it's time to take the breath away. Then the person goes to sleep and leaves his family and wakes up in heaven in the arms of Father Abraham . . .

As tired as he was I could not get him to go to sleep last night. With sharp words from Joseph he was quiet, but he lay there wide-eyed, even when we went to bed.

With another child on the way—and mad Archelaus barking over Judea—I send Joseph off to the pilgrim

Feast of Booths and stay here at home, with some ambivalence.

On the one hand, I long to step inside the Lord's city, to worship on the holy ground. I long to see Elizabeth, Zechariah, and their John, to hear Elizabeth's heart.

On the other hand, it is easier for me if Joseph goes ahead into Bethlehem, spying out the land, bringing me back a report: Are there giants there for me to fear?

Mary, where is your faith? Why do you even consider hiding behind him—just because it makes for a smoother journey?

A blue day: body-sick, laden with this wombed child; mind-sick, confined by the strictures of the present, the promised future always walled away.

Jesus is like warm wax, imprinted with my mood. After his nap he climbed up on my knee. His cheek to mine, he silently offered a comfort almost parental, then said, "Mama, don't be sad. Think about the Sabbath. It always comes back."

Joseph back from Jerusalem and a side trip out to Bethlehem. He went to Rachel's door, didn't wait for her to hear that he was in town and come over to Uncle Samuel's. She has another child, a girl still at her breast.

Joseph said she was quiet, restrained, acting as if she was afraid—maybe of her own emotion. He didn't stay long: She seemed to desire his—our—condolences, but at the same time she didn't want to stand face to face with pain.

She wanted explanations. Why did we leave? Did we know her Benjamin was in danger? Why hadn't we warned them? Why wasn't there escape for all?

He left her in tears.

"Joseph, did she ask of my well-being or of Jesus'? Did you tell her I carry another?"

"No, Mary. I'm sure the questions just slipped her mind."

Jesus begs to sleep on the roof even when we think it's too cold for comfort. We're still saying okay, though that won't last much longer. (I could be so cozy if I snuggled in a cradle between two warm bodies.)

I opened my eyes this morning and Jesus was awake. Staring at the sky, listening for the morning songs and waiting for the sun. When he saw that I was awake he whispered for me to listen and be quiet so as not to disturb Joseph.

How much power I have over him—I suppose any parent over any child. Without real intention I establish these patterns—games, maybe?—that become rituals owned by him more than me. It's frightening—and exciting.

My first pains hit hard and have passed. Mother called Joseph in from the shop to take Jesus out, to Granddad Jacob's and the care of Little Mary. Jesus kept holding back, not wanting to leave me, sensing the fuss.

So a boychild is given us. A healthy child, with a red face and no hair. You forget how tiny and perfectly knit . . .

James, he will be called.

Sat all morning cracking and separating walnuts to serve at the circumcision feast. Tired of the tedium I turned my thoughts to the days of the Lord's creations. What did I see? On three of the six days His acts were of separation: the light from the dark, the waters in the sky from the waters on the earth, the sea from the dry ground.

And how much of my life concerns acts of separation?

walnuts from shells
wheat from chaff
vegetables from weeds
cheese from whey
Jews from Gentiles
clean from unclean
men from women
sheep from wool
wool fibers from other wool fibers
the living from the dead

So I sat and separated more contentedly. Not with any thought that my act was like the Lord's. (His act changed the very nature of the earth. Take light and dark. If dark prevailed before the first day, the act of pulling light out from the dark cut off the overwhelming power of darkness. Figure this: A small lamp flame can pierce the darkness like a nail through a board. But darkness has no such power.

The comparable image might be a shadow—which only hints at breaking through the light.)

In separating, the Most High created. In separating, I make order I can live with.

Every morning, every night, Joseph faces the city and repeats the standard by which we live: Listen, Israel, love the Lord the one God; teach the commands to your children . . .

What does it mean for me this day?

Both Joseph and I have been drilling hard—teaching Jesus the commandments. He's never said them perfectly, always stumbling and needing prodding, but today he looked up and said, "I have the commandments all locked up in my heart." His granddad would be proud.

Leah says Heaven has seen fit to dry her river. The look on her face is this: hope skewed by pain—like someone who is smiling but whose cheek and chin are paralyzed on one side. You can identify the intent of a smile, but the look is off.

Jesus staring off into space this afternoon.

"What are you thinking about?"

"I can't tell you, because if I do, it will all come out of my head."

PART 6

Separations

He found him in a desert land, and in the howling waste of the wilderness; he encircled him, he cared for him, he kept him as the apple of his eye. Like an eagle that stirs up its nest, that flutters over its young, spreading out its wings, catching them, bearing them on its pinions, the Lord alone did lead him.

—*Moses*

James is weaned. I am unbound. Cause for celebration.

There's always something to celebrate. Didn't God intend it so, saying "It is good" after every day of creation?

And besides, day-upon-day life would grow endlessly dreary if one did not make the choice to celebrate transitions. Choose to see them as births instead of deaths, though what beginning isn't tainted with grief over some ending?

How to melt a mother's heart: "Mom, will you sing us one of the songs of Zion?"

This Passover, Mother says she wants to go down to visit Elizabeth. It is good for her to go, and I can manage the children here alone.

She will bring me back word of their life, which seems so far away from mine here.

Please . . . Jesus scrounged two sticks from Joseph just as he was closing up the shop before the feast days. He waited until morning—after Joseph had left town—and now he is playing drums, banging on every inanimate object within his reach.

Even animate objects: Thinking himself clever he walked up behind me this evening, tap tapping on my shoulders.

I gave in to his enthusiasm and picked up my flute and let him (try to) beat out—on the wooden chest, not my back—the rhythm of our favorite songs.

But tomorrow I will change my tune, neither encouraging or discouraging this, hoping he will tire of it quickly. There's my own sanity to consider, and I know Joseph will have little patience for this when he gets home from Jerusalem. (Say nothing of my poor mother . . .)

Mother's story of Elizabeth: If someone can be both chronically exhausted and exhilarated, it is she. She doesn't forget her miracle. She lives in praise.

And yet, after one day there Mother was thanking the Most High that Elizabeth's prancing John spent his mornings at the synagogue school; how could Elizabeth cope otherwise? It's not, Mother says, that he's a disobedient child; it's that he has so much energy and such an overbearing presence.

Elizabeth was full of questions of our welfare and ways, sending word that she waits and hopes and prays for the sons' coming of age.

Joseph saw Rachel again. Each time, he says, she is cool toward him, and yet there's always something about the exchange that makes him feel it's important that he knock on her door when he returns to town. Yes, she asked of me.

Friend Judith has died after two full days of labor

and no delivery. The midwife says she knew the baby was dead but never told Judith. This being her first, she didn't know the signs and died in hope.

Jesus—five and heading out my door, down the street to the synagogue school.

I've prepared him too well: He was excited. Once the teacher saw him and told him where to sit—between Clopas and Neriah—Jesus didn't look back at me. I stood at the door—longer than the teacher liked—waiting for my own child to turn around and acknowledge my existence. Just a quick glance, a silent, "Hey, Mom, I'll miss you but I'll be okay. Thanks for walking me over. See you later."

Too much to ask. James and I went home alone.

Jesus, before going to sleep: "If you rope your dreams together, you can make a great story."

On his way home from school Jesus stopped off at Leah's and she gave him two eggs to bring home to me. He put them in his pocket and . . .

Sometimes I wonder whose child he is.

Every morning as he walks out the door with his friends who have stopped by for him, I silently pray an extra measure of grace on his day.

The favorite game of every generation: David and

Goliath. Jesus and his friends are playing it, throwing stones at a sycamore limb.

"Joseph, soon he's going to be asking for a sling-shot. You know that son of Simeon the tanner has never been right since he was hit in the head . . .

"They shouldn't be throwing stones. They're getting stronger and their aim is better and the stones are bouncing back off the tree. Someone's going to get hurt.

"And as for the slingshot, we have to be ready to say no. They're not toys. I don't care what the other parents think."

He listens to me. I know he hears what I'm saying. But he doesn't respond.

"Mom, what is lust?"

"Go to the shop and ask your father to explain it. But if there are any customers there, you mustn't interrupt. Wait and ask when they're gone."

Joseph and Jesus are making me something. Sometimes when I go into the shop Joseph quickly shuffles boards so they're awkwardly askew. Jesus starts talking real fast, trying to divert my attention and keep me away from the back corner. Joseph just grunts at me, discouraging my presence. I'll play their game and not act suspicious.

Their stealth and camaraderie pleases me.

Jesus is seven years old. Is it insane that yesterday, at the synagogue, I looked over the crowd in the gallery—the women and children of our village—and wondered, *Whose daughter will be good enough for him to marry?*

Tonight Joseph, Father Jacob, and Jesus walked in from the shop carrying a walnut loom. Jesus was beaming—proud of his work, tickled that I seemed surprised.

Jacob left right away. Joseph stayed in the background of this presentation, washing for dinner, pretending not to pay much attention—though of course he was.

I don't much like to weave. Would rather spin or cook. Maybe this will provide inspiration.

Joseph and I argued tonight. I mean a real argument. If it's happened before I've chosen not to remember it—our volleying words spoken in raised tones.

He is whittling Jesus a slingshot. Says playing David and Goliath is a part of growing up. I've got to learn to deal with reality. Perhaps if I'd had brothers I would understand . . .

Sarah's Laughter

No woman yearned more
for fruit than I,
when my blossom bloomed red.
But pollen, so plentiful,
might as well have rained
on a rock made of granite.
And now my pleasurable flower
is faded, shriveled,
and, besides, bees can't swarm
from an empty hive.

"Mom, no one can play. Will you play hopscotch with me? Ple-e-e-ease?"

"Play it with James, dear."

"He's too little. He always trips up."

"I don't remember how to play."

"I'll teach you."

"I'm really very busy here. Can't you see?"

"You play with me and then I'll help you."

"You help me first and then I'll play . . ."

"What if someone sees me? What if an important customer comes by and sees the wife of Joseph playing hopscotch?"

"Grandma can watch the gate. Mom you have to. You promised."

"One game, Jesus. Just one game."

I played three.

No. Not true. A better mother than I would have played three.

I played one and then threw up, sick with the new life I carry.

A family's history: It's a cord that winds and knots itself around a household. My years with Joseph—the accumulation of our shared laughter and tears, silences and conversations, sighs and groans—would bind us to each other even if we were not bound by the Lord's command.

And, praise Heaven, the children (fruit grown in the wake of passion faded like a flower) pull the knots tighter, two becoming one.

This third child quickened today. A comforting feeling that all is well.

Rabbi came by the shop, tousled Jesus' hair, and said how much he looked like his dad—Joseph. Joseph smiled and said, "He's quite a boy, praise be to God."

Actually he does have Joseph's eyes. (I hardly remember the look of Joseph's cheeks and chin, before his beard came in.) Maybe it is a little joke to make us laugh.

Little Mary (I must stop calling her that) was betrothed today—to Eli the older brother of Jesus' friend Clopas. A nice boy for her. May her future be blessed.

So this child is a girl, a tiny Elizabeth I pray to be as holy as her aunt. Each birth is easier. Maybe I fear each less. Maybe the moon pulls harder.

I don't feel fully prepared for raising a girl, though I was brought up with them. Yes, I'd thought of the possibility that this one would be my kind, and yet experience had taught me to expect a boy. And who doesn't want a quiverful of boys?

Anyway, a girl it is. The question needn't be answered for years but I ask it now: Will I teach my daughter to write and read?

Don't play games with rhetorical questions. Yes, of course you will.

Every spring Jesus gets more taken up in the drama of the Purim service. The older boys take the lead, acting out their righteous anger at wicked Haman. At every mention of Haman's name the children stomp their feet, louder and louder until he hangs from his own schemed gallows.

Hating evil, it's so easy when you're a child. The hate is not colored with fear.

Tedious, tedium. Stack the days one upon another. It is easy to be so mired in the present that you forget the wonders in your own past, no less dramatic than the stories of the prophets and kings.

Reminder: You are a woman seen and chosen by the Almighty who found favor in your heart—willing to please and obey His word.

Tedious, tedium. Would you think the childhood years of a nation's deliverer would be as quiet as life in Nazareth?

I asked Joseph: Should we send Jesus—not yet, he's far too young, but in time—to Jerusalem to study with the scholars? Should we someday—even further down the road, *years* from now—push him into the angry arms of the Zealots who secretly plot the routing of Rome?

He didn't answer for a long time. "Mary, we've never been given much notice, but when major changes have been important, we've received word. We've known . . ."

Lord, guide me—and Joseph—as we prepare this boy for manhood.

What a fuss today. Laban, son of Simon two streets over, came home announcing that he was taking Susannah, wild daughter of Simon the hill shepherd, as wife.

Simon (two streets over) was so angry the whole town got in on it: He bought a barrel of fruit and smashed one melon at a time in the middle of market street. Of course he didn't do this in silence. The message was clear: Her children will not be heirs of mine. "May they be scattered like the seeds of these melons."

Laban wasn't there to watch the scene, though his mother was—sobbing (her youngest daughter clinging to her skirt), as if it were Laban's funeral.

Jesus stayed long after the crowd had broken up. At dinner he didn't eat much. And in the evening he threw up. When I asked he admitted he'd slurped some of the melon pieces. He couldn't remember how many.

Joseph piped in with the wisdom of Jesus ben Sira: My son, test your constitution . . . overeating makes one sick.

I know, Jesus said. I know.

Is there nothing new under the sun? Mother's lesson, and her mother's, has become my own: Today I took the children and went visiting, to Sepphoris to see the new baby of Eli and Sister Mary. (I'll call her that for now, instead of Little Mary.) When we got within sight of her house and I exclaimed, "We're here," James ran ahead right into the house, through the open door, without knocking or asking to be invited in.

Sister Mary was ever so cordial but right there on the spot I corrected James, giving Mother's explanation of God's good manners: In Eden, though He well knew where shamed Adam was hiding, God asked, "Adam, where are you?" His lesson was that we are always to announce ourselves before entering another's house.

As I admonished him I heard my mother's voice, yet coming from my mouth. Her hovering concern that things be done right. I was surprised the recognition didn't horrify me. I actually found it humorous. Maybe comforting.

Her tack worked to teach me. Shouldn't it work to teach my own?

Jesus is ten years old today. He gets so excited about birthdays. On his way out to school, he took the stairs down to the lower level in one long leap—landing in a heap.

"What's the big rush?" I asked, and it's the question that's stayed with me all day.

When you're young you're always trying to give age a little push, trying to force it so you can be a little older. But then . . .

Combing out my hair this morning I found a white strand. A tare among the wheat.

I pulled it out.

What's the big rush?

Jesus very quiet last night and this morning. When Clopas came by to walk him to school, Jesus was up on the roof, not responding to my calls.

I sent Clopas on ahead, James tagging along, and went upstairs. He was sitting stone still, huddled in a tight ball, knees to chin.

"What's wrong?"

Silence. Staring at the horizon, not me. "Nothing."

"You heard the first school horn. Clopas has already been here and gone. Are you ill?"

"No."

"Is there a problem at school?"

"Please leave me alone."

"Do you want me to get your father?"

"No. I'll catch up. In a minute. Leave me alone. The baby's crawling up the steps. You better go see about her. She might fall."

Yes, once he mentioned it I could hear that she was, and what kind of a mother wouldn't run down to tend her, and, once down, I decided it best to stay down, give him a few minutes.

The second school horn rang. He was late and would be chastised.

Yelled upstairs, "Jesus, I'm going out to the shop to get your father. If you're not ill, you must go to school. Now."

Still not looking at me (is it too much to hope for: some everything's-okay-Mom assurance?), he ran down the stairs and out the gate.

Told Joseph today that I want to go with him this spring, to Jerusalem for the Passover feast. Mother says she can handle the children here. (I will wean Elizabeth a few months younger than I did the boys.) Jesus is ten—old enough to help out.

I asked for one favor: that we be able to visit both Elizabeth in the hill country and—yes, I said it—Rachel in Bethlehem. I need to see them both.

Leave for Judea in three days. I'm going by choice; I should be excited.

I am excited . . . but apprehensive . . . and not quite sure I want to be away from my children, my baby, for two weeks.

The feeling: I need to do this—more than want to do this.

"Joseph, I want to take the myrrh and give it to Rachel as a gift of consolation."

The whistling stopped and the eyes bore in.

"It won't bring Benjamin back to her. You're trying to atone for something you can't possibly make right."

"It's a gesture."

"An expensive one."

"Please."

"Mary . . ."

With little more conversation Joseph dug up the myrrh and packed it to take.

All I remember of last night's dream: I stood at Rachel's door waiting for her to answer my knock. In front of me, with two hands so I'm sure not to drop it, I held—not the sealed jar of precious ointment but—a soldier's battle shield, golden, protecting my heart against the sword I was sure I'd see in Rachel's fist.

I knew she was home, in the backyard. She kept calling, "I'm coming. I'm coming." But I waited and waited and woke up before she appeared.

In Bethlehem. No dream. The real greeting: I stood at Rachel's door, praying peace, two hands holding the vial of myrrh against my breast. A six-year-old daughter quickly opened the door, looked me over, ran back inside.

From the big room Rachel—tending twin toddler boys—saw me. Froze.

Neither did I move, except for shoving the myrrh into the air between us. "Shalom, Rachel."

It was no rushing—gushing—wind, but she came to the door and invited me in, keeping her children in front of her, bunched in her skirt.

"I want you to have this." The gift was getting heavy—as if it *were* a soldier's shield.

She didn't offer to unburden me, so I set the offering down on the wooden chest.

"You remember—the visitors from the East? They brought gifts . . . myrrh. For you. A remembrance, of Benjamin, from Joseph and me . . . I'm sorry . . . And who can explain the ways of the Almighty?"

Here's what I read in her face: She wanted to be angry but recognized the futility of the stance. Can anger raise the dead?

She wanted to run from me, as my presence prompted the pain of another's absence. But she did not hide, ultimately being a prisoner of hope.

So in the end she drank my comfort. Tentative small talk giving way to tentative smiles . . . to tentative tears . . . to weary grief flowing like a deep, wide river.

And in comforting her, I was forgiven by her. For what? For heeding the call. For ever setting foot in this town. For being blessed with fortune—the hand of death passing over my oldest son while striking hers.

At my insistence she kept the myrrh.

A gesture. It can never atone.

Dreamt of Eve, though the face was clearly Rachel's. She—Eve—was sitting against a fig tree, holding a dead baby I knew was Abel. She was so solitary and distraught that I sat down and enfolded her in my arms.

Eve still on my mind. What did she have in Eden?

Surrounded by Eden
Eve hungered for more
and more she ate than she knew:
the knowledge that what she'd had
was all there ever would be.

On our way back north. We left the Nazareth caravan to stop off at Elizabeth's. She walks, but with great pain; she grieves that she will never again get to the City. This struck me more than anything else in our visit. Being considerably older than Mother, she is of an age where age is an issue.

I will never again go here, enjoy this, that. Though it is not a totally new realization (I will never again be a virgin, see Father, . . .), it rarely treads through my thoughts.

But when I am old—it will tramp at will. And even now it stakes a claim: I will never again see Elizabeth.

Oh, her John—eleven years old: intense, well versed in Scripture, a loner. I can't quite imagine him laughing or telling a joke.

One week out of four: Don't touch me. Unclean. Don't sit on my chair. Unclean. Stay away. Dirty. Unfit.

Am I as unclean to Joseph as the Gentile Romans are to me?

This uncleanness is still on my mind, especially today as I washed stained linen rags.

What did Isaiah say? That my righteous acts—even his, he admitted in incredible humility—were as these woman's clotted cloths unclean unclean unclean.

If that is the case we stand at the mercy of Heaven.

In the synagogue I try to compare Jesus to the other boys his age, his friends Clopas and Neriah. He is generally more attentive, though sometimes I can't tell if he's listening or daydreaming, off in his own world.

But then when Joseph quizzes him in the afternoon, he knows the answers to the questions as well as I.

Such a toothache I could not have imagined had it not been throbbing at the back of my own jaw. But what is worse, a toothache or a gaping, bleeding hole in your mouth? There comes a point when you lose

fear of the dentist's pliers because you know they are
the promise of relief. You must walk straight into the
slaughteryard—in hope of freedom.

As every pilgrim feast approaches Jesus begs to
go along to Jerusalem—as many of his school
friends do. (To hear him tell it, you'd think he was
the only eleven-year-old boy not allowed to make
the trip to the temple. But I know a number of families who will not let their boys go until they are con-
sidered men—or at least until the demon Archelaus
is dead. Jerusalem is no place for the children of
this generation.)

Are we being too protective?

The calendar makers say the moon has gotten ahead
of us. Adar is ending. Nisan, the month of Passover,
should be coming in. But the lambs are too late and
too small. The barley fields are far from ripe. So this is
the year of thirteen months, two Adars, Adar followed by Veadar.

An extra month before the Passover. What will I do
with it? What a silly question. I will grind my family's
flour, bake their bread, and serve their table. I will
spin threads and weave cloths. I will prod, shush, and
herd the children. Listen to their lessons. Teach them
mine. I will daughter my mother and wife my husband, as I have every month for the last . . .

It's not a silly question. There's an extra month
here, so what will I do to redeem it? I will show an
extra measure of kindness to (1) the family living here
under our roof, (2) the women in my circle: Mary,

Leah, Rebekah, (3) my sister Salome. Yes, I will arrange for an overnight trip to Capernaum, taking Mother and the children to see her.

But there's something else. I miss the wonders discovered by Mary the Dawdler, who seems to have fallen asleep; it's time she were shaken awake, like a lazy child.

Jesus is jumping out of his skin with excitement that he may go with us to Jerusalem to Passover—a year before his rightful manhood, at thirteen. We've never explained that violent Archelaus was a prime factor in his staying here with Grandmother each spring—when some mothers in town will travel with their children. And we didn't say that Archelaus's recent deposition from power was reason for our grant of privilege.

("We think James is old enough now to stay here with Grandmother. This year you may go to the feasts, Jerusalem. But the privilege comes with responsibility: You must care for the lamb we are taking with us.")

Come, let us go up to the mountain of the Lord, that He may teach us His ways.

Setting up camp, our second night on the road. Jesus fussing over the lamb as if it were a baby. He will be a good father, which reminds me that I haven't written of my latest suspicion. Yes. Wean one, conceive one. The story of a woman's life.

Every year I should have the thrill of seeing—and hearing and smelling—this city as if for the first time and through the eyes of youth.

The horde. The blood. The smoke . . .

Jesus and Joseph met Zechariah today and his John, who (Jesus reported) didn't stand still the whole hour they were together. If he wasn't pacing, he was pounding a fist into a palm or tapping with the ball of his foot.

Joseph reported that for a while the boys listened to the men's conversation; eventually they struck up their own.

My questioning: "Jesus, what did you and John talk about?"

"I asked him what he knew about various temple teachers."

Elizabeth holds on to life, confined to the house. Joseph says there is no extra time to visit her.

Heaven be merciful. Jesus is gone. We've canvassed the whole caravan and no one has seen him since we broke up camp this morning. All day I've thought him with Joseph and the men—or surely with Clopas and Neriah, whom I hadn't seen all day; Joseph assumed he, still a child after all, was with me and the women.

We will rise before the sun and head back. Everyone agrees he can't be traveling ahead of us. We'll ask and look for him in every group we meet tomorrow. He must have wandered away from the camp, and once away (he is prone to distraction) become confused, every camp looking like all the others.

Once he realized we'd left, he would have known

(I pray, I pray) to head for Jericho, to cross the river and head north on the main road. So we're sure to find him—by noon, I'd say.

I asked Joseph how much money he had with him and suggested he borrow some. Bad move. "Woman, if you'd tend to your mothering half as well as you tend to my affairs, we wouldn't be in this mess." Stomped off, I think to borrow money.

He's right, though. It's all my fault.

Back in the city tonight, and no Jesus. We looked. We asked. We called his name. By now most of the camps are broken up. People are on their way home.

We got pity. Food. Stares.

No answers. No hint of recognition. No angel messages.

This place is a maze. He could be anywhere—and paralyzed with fear.

In the morning Joseph will go out to Bethlehem. Jesus knows we have people there. He may have asked around and figured he'd be safe there. I will retrace our steps of the last week, inquiring of shopkeepers, travelers, anyone.

Day and night, Lord, I call to You. Turn Your ear to my cry, for my soul is full of trouble. Turn Your ear to the cry of my lost boy, whose child-soul is surely more troubled than mine.

No Jesus. No sleep. No revealing dreams.

Panic—tempered by the task of the search. I can't afford to fall apart.

Guilt: my utter lack of responsibility. I, given such a privileged charge, have let him—still a boy—slip out of my shelter. Will I find forgiveness for such gross negligence?

I can hardly believe my boldness today. Twice I approached Roman soldiers (One was older, a seasoned sergeant. Who knows—maybe the very man who speared Benjamin in search for Jesus?) asking if they'd seen a lost twelve-year-old. The younger soldier laughed and mocked. "Be gone." The older man didn't laugh. He said he was sorry, but he hadn't.

I must hold on until Jesus is found. Learn the lesson of Mother Sarah's untimely death: Assuming the worst (that her Isaac was dead) she died before she could know the whole story (that he lived).

Surely Jesus is alive.

How long will the Name remain silent?

In the temple, talking to the rabbis. Without the slightest concern for our worry. Surprised at our anger. Oblivious to the world around him. Just writing these words makes my eyes tear so that I cannot see to continue . . .

Praise to the Name for leading us to him. Praise to the Name for his being tended and attentive—though from what I saw it was the rabbis who were rapt.

But . . . I can hardly contain my frustration—seasoned with relief and maybe embarrassment.

"Didn't you know that I would be here—tending my Father's affairs?"—as if this (our parental panic as well as our separation) were *all* our fault.

On the way home I laid down the law: From now on I want more details—who he's with and where he's going and when he's coming home. No. He won't tell me when he's coming home. I'll tell him when he's expected. Do you understand, young man? Do you hear me?

We've let the reins lie too loose and they've got to be pulled in.

"Didn't you know I'd be here tending my Father's affairs?"

Wait, go back to the angel's announcement of the coming child: "He will be called the Son of the Most High." Maybe not right at first, but for years now I've thought of him as being fathered by no man—being fatherless.

Have I missed something? Was Jesus saying something important to me?

With a pained silence Jesus is unhappy with my short rein, my hovering. He answers my questions but with no more than the required information.

For the second time in a week, Jesus has cried out in the middle of the night, as if with nightmares.

"Did you have a bad dream last night?"

"I guess so."

"What was it about?"

"The priest killing our lamb."

PART 7

Remembrances

Remember your Creator in the days of
your youth, before the days of trouble
come and the years approach when you
will say, "I find no pleasure in them."

—*The Preacher*

A child in a womb, a gourd on a vine.

A woman in this condition is like a wild gourd that grows round, fat, heavy and bursts open when ripe. And there's the taste and effect of the gourd's medicinal pulp: bitter and purgative.

Mother asks that she be able to weave Jesus' prayer shawl, as his thirteenth birthday approaches. Despite my prejudices against the task, I had wanted to weave this, as is the custom. But Mother is bringing up old regrets: her not being able to officiate at his birth. This denial of privilege (she reasons) gives her a claim to weaving his prayer covering.

I will honor her and her request. A small sacrifice will win a great satisfaction—for her but in turn for me.

Jesus: "But Mother, you don't understand."

Will I have to listen to this for the next five years?

Another birth, though this one harder than any and a girl, Lydia. She came face-first, actually lips-first. Abigail the midwife let out a squeal when she first touched the baby. The little sucker pulled Abigail's finger right into her mouth.

I remember Joseph coming into the room after the

other births. His eyes went to the baby and then to me. But this time he looked first at my face, as if he'd been waiting to look after me and my welfare more than that of his child. His look was relief, concern, affection. Neither pride nor disappointment in this being a daughter.

Our silent exchange lasted but a second—his interest quickly focused on Lydia—but for that moment we were as much one as two could ever be.

Yesterday Jesus split open his thumb hammering. Came in for balm and bandage trying to hold back tears like a man, though the boy won out. I held his shoulders and let him cry, wondering if it would be the last time.

He's sure to lose his thumbnail.

This holy one grows up here in Nazareth studying with our rabbis of no acclaim, eating bread kneaded by my palm, learning how to earn an honest living—joining corners of hewn wood.

King David grew up in a sheepfield, as did prophet Amos. The prophets—Isaiah, Jeremiah—even Moses, felt unprepared and were, except for the anointing of the Spirit. All this I know and yet I wonder still: Are we doing enough? Should we send him away, as the rabbi advises?

I can ask the question here in these private papers, but actual good-byes . . . That I am not ready to face.

Jesus—thirteen, beardless yet counted among the

bearded men reading, praying, teaching at the synagogue. He read on the Sabbath and gave his commentary, quite extraordinary for a youth.

But I'm his mother, so maybe this warrants an outside opinion.

To send him to Jerusalem or not to send him? We make no decision and yet no decision is itself a decision.

Joseph wonders why God seems so silent in recent years. Will we be given no more clear instruction?

Maybe we will send him down for one winter, next winter when he is fourteen—that much older.

Spending evenings on the roof and sleeping there these hot days. Last night the whole family hunted the skies for the constellations. Fun.

Joseph and Jesus back from Sepphoris, where they put in a new door frame for Eli. They're both agitated tonight, though I can't get much out of them. Has something to do with Judas the Zealot and his rebellious schemes against Herod Antipas. "It's a man's worry, Mary. Don't bother yourself with questions."

It's a man's worry. I think there's trouble a-foot—swords and blood—and I'm supposed to close my eyes, close my mouth, and pretend I don't want to know about it.

Well, if I were honest a part of me does want to turn my face to the wall. I am my father's daughter. But I don't like having information withheld from me as if I were a child.

Jesus, and James too but especially Jesus, enjoys entertaining his little sisters. His patience is long; his laughter, light. Last night he sat in the middle of the floor, a jester mesmerizing a court.

The wooden ball Joseph whittled for Jesus is still part of the scene, though no longer decorated with my contribution of color.

I have been married fourteen years—the years of Jacob's labor for Laban—or was it his labor for Rachel? It has to be the best love story in the Scriptures: Jacob waiting out the best years of his life, working off Laban's treachery, for the woman he loved.

For fourteen years Joseph has been good to me; he's still the righteous man I married. Praise the Name. I cannot imagine life without him.

But today when I add up all the days and nights we've been together, I marvel more at Jacob's love than ours.

A herd of Roman soldiers rode through town today, heading north toward Sepphoris, driving like Jehu. It can only mean trouble.

Heaven be merciful. The soldiers have torched Sepphoris, the whole town fallen in on itself or falling from the sky as mournful ash. Joseph has gone to look for his sister Mary. He took Jesus, made James stay here.

They've been gone all day.

Jesus walked in carrying a terrified orphaned boy less than two years old, unweaned, unscathed. As usual no details but Joseph assures me his mother is dead. He didn't ask; it's just assumed that we'll house the boy until we can find other relatives.

Mary and her little boy Taphath are safe, back with Joseph's parents. But her husband Eli is dead, along with nearly every Jewish man in the town. Those not speared or maimed then burned to char hang on crosses along the road—or under guard wait an emptied cross. Joseph says Jesus retched at the sight . . .

Eli didn't suffer long. It's little consolation.

If it weren't a serious matter, it would seem like a game: We address the boy by name after name; he doesn't respond.

Will I have enough milk for two?

The boy's eyes stayed with us when we called him Simon, and then the Sepphoris widows—now our widows—confirmed that that's his name. They say they have seen none of his relatives. Mary is fortunate; some natives lost husband, father, brothers, sons, all.

Nazareth's resources are stretched to breaking. Some of our own men are being arrested.

I haven't ventured out of town. The crosses. There are long-suffered wounds I can't bear to see.

Simon wails or whimpers. He eats a little porridge but will not take my breast. Falls asleep at night only when walked—and walked—face buried in Jesus' chest.

Dream: Jesus maybe four. Separated from me, shopping on the near end of main street in Sepphoris. I've looked for him long enough to be panicked, then a scurry and the Roman cavalry rides in, torching stacks of woolens, bins of grain. They spill oil on and light wood piles. Then more soldiers, spearing babies out of their mother's arms. One is Rachel but I can't stop to comfort her.

I suddenly know where Jesus is hiding—in the far corner of the temple, which has somehow been displaced from Jerusalem to Galilee.

I run back into town. I dodge the deaths. He's there unattended and searching the crowd, looking for me, looking for him. When he sees me, he clings to my neck sobbing and inconsolable, still afraid I might be lost forever.

Joseph wakes me up, shakes me off. What's wrong with you? You're choking me.

The unclaimed boy is one of us. We will make room at table, room on the floor, and I pray that there will be room in my affections for a son not mine yet mine.

When he is still young—fifteen—Clopas will marry Mary. May they be blessed with a boychild, a son for Eli.

On Joseph's Work
Love Poem Written While Weaving
"The sleep of a laborer is sweet,
whether he eats little or much"

—The Preacher

Blisters, splinters, sweat: Adam's curse
distilled on your hairy flesh, coarse
like a cloak but warmer
than wool woven tight to ward
off a night's harsh chill.

The dinner lesson: One day two sheep came upon a destitute man, starving for lack of food. If he just had a bag of wool to sell at the market, he could feed himself and his family. But this man, not a man of force, would not take the sheep's wool without their consent. He asked: "Could you spare me your wool on this fine spring day?"

One sheep took pity on the beggar and gave up his wool coat. The other said, "No, I need it myself."

That night the two sheep—one shaven clean and the other woolly warm—had to swim across a river. But the two did not fare equally well: While the generous sheep swam easily to the far shore, the miserly one drowned for the weight of his treasure.

The catch of the story: Jesus told it, not Joseph.

Simon continues to find more consolation in Jesus than in me, though I am the boy's tender by day. We all agree that we will wait one more year before Jesus goes down to Jerusalem. When he is fifteen.

I asked Jesus who was his favorite character in the Scriptures. He said Moses, and I quickly reminded him of the song he used to beg me to sing—the horse and rider. (Actually, I burst out singing it.)

I was more amused than he, so I got serious and asked him why Moses.

He gave an odd answer: Because he was chosen.

I shall have to remember to ask him again in a few years.

Joseph—and Jesus—back from Jerusalem and the Feast of Booths. He inquired at the temple and was told that Zechariah and Elizabeth are dead—she first and then he within the month. And the son—they said—had run away, not to be seen since the day of his father's burial.

I told Mother—and Joseph—that we must keep a lookout. John's never been here but he knows he has relatives in Nazareth. I mean, he could just show up here in town one day soon, and of course we'd take him in for a few years until he was of a marrying age . . .

I said this with a heart willing—but wishing that John's restless youth would be tamed under the roof of some other.

All right. It's time to admit what I've been hiding even from myself. Write it: I'm carrying another child.

Now, go to the roof, open your mouth, and tell Joseph how blessed he is. Go.

I didn't go then. Right then I cried.

I told him in the middle of the night, which, these days, seems the only ready time for personal conversation. He seemed pleased. But this morning, as is sometimes the case, I wasn't sure he'd remembered what I'd told him.

How can one little spider weave such an elaborate network that threatens to take over a whole corner of my house? With a broom I knocked it down, and a few days later the threads are back, tiny fishnets floating in the air. Tonight I feel as if I've spent my whole life fighting and losing a battle against spider webs—and dust and sand. Minuscule enemies that refuse to retreat, that refuse to die though I beat them with no mercy.

I just want to sleep.

Lord, have mercy.

Joseph is starting to lose his hair, though I wouldn't think of pointing this out to him. He spends no time in front of a mirror; maybe he won't notice.

If the recession continues, maybe I should remind the children of Elisha's wild-bear curse. Give them good reason to show due respect.

Yes, we will send Jesus to Jerusalem for the winter.

Deliverance

It is time.
My body's clock gongs
your salvation's hour.
The water has left the pasture and

flowed toward the river's mouth.
Follow or you will wither
in the desert that remains.
I will bleed for you
on this your first dark journey
but, in time, when life pushes you
headlong through black canyons
the wounds will be your own.
May you learn early:
At the end light always shines.
It is here, child;
the time is come.
Breathe.

A double portion from the Lord. Twin boys, hard to tell apart. I should have guessed there were two, with the unparalleled punching and kicking.

To be named Joseph and Judas.

Will I have enough milk? Will I have the strength to withstand the Lord's good grace?

Good-bye to Jesus, going down to the Feast of Booths and staying three months. Now there's nothing to worry about. Joseph will arrange his lodging and care.

Had kept a mulberry-dipped tie around the swaddled loins of Joseph, the first-born twin. He apparently kicked it off; Simon apparently dragged it off as a toy. Elizabeth apparently picked up one of the babies—Judas, she thought—and danced him around the room. Then Lydia poked and prodded at the

other, so that he wiggled to the far side of the mat.
Then they realized that neither baby was wearing the
purple tie. Then they got confused and panicked and
by the time Mother and I got in on the act Lydia was
crying and Elizabeth was yelling and neither had any
idea which boy was which . . .

I'm quite sure I have remarked them correctly,
knowing them apart from the way each feeds. But an
unsettling doubt has been introduced. What if the
older grows up as the younger and the younger as
the older? What if one is Judas to me but Joseph to the
Most High . . . ?

Woke this morning convinced I should fast today,
for Jesus—absent in body but present in my mind.

The sun sets now, hunger gnaws as Mother stirs a
stew, and yet there's no real contest: Mind prevails
over body, and prayer rises like an herbal fragrance to
the nostrils of God.

Jesus walked in the door this afternoon eager for
greetings, especially from the children who flocked to
his knees, then arms.

Will this regret—for having sent him off, for thinking that learning would prepare him for a leader's
life—pass quickly or remain permanently?

In three months he has changed. It's not that he's a
stranger; he's always fought an inner battle that we

are not privy to. But the battle is hotter now, like the sun in midsummer.

Tonight he's gone off to the cliff, jealous Simon clung to his back.

A story came out tonight at dinner: On Jesus' way back home to Nazareth, two Roman soldiers approached, pulled him out of the traveling party, and for sport demanded that he carry a saddle bag for a mile—heading back east.

He relayed the account with no evident indignation, as if he were telling us about watching woodcutters fell a tree.

Sister Mary has married young Clopas whose beard is hardly in. She seems content; he, nervous, wary of the prospects of inheriting a ready-made family.

At the party Jesus loosened up considerably, enjoying his first role as groomsman. In what—three years? —it will be he taking a wife.

Dream: Within hours of his birth, my baby, a boy, though not one as distinguished from the others—independent beyond his age—refused to take my breast. I started to sob, knowing the meaning of his willful rejection: that a child's life goal, even reason for being, is to separate himself from me—to leave me behind.

The sadness lingers.

Joseph's dinner tale, an exhortation for his sons to mind the character of the girls they dream on—and maybe an exhortation to his blossoming daughter listening in: A righteous man took a righteous wife but alas the woman was barren and for that reason, in time, they divorced. The husband married again, this time a wicked woman, and cast off his holy life for evil ways. The wife, on the other hand, married a wicked man who was soon acclaimed in the town for his piety.

Now, sons, what is the lesson of this story?

Jesus: "The lesson is yours, Dad. Find your sons wives righteous as Hannah."

James: "But pretty as Queen Esther."

Sister Mary has birthed a healthy boy, Joseph. I will call him Joseph the Younger.

Did I hear what I think I heard? James teasing Jesus—for being sweet on Benjamin's daughter Abigail.

Mother, reminiscing of Aunt Elizabeth, reminded me of her consuming awareness of her miracle.

Am I always aware of my miracle? I fear days go by and I haul water, pull weeds, dry tears, grind flour . . . more aware of the present—the coughing of a child with a runny nose; the texture of dough between my fingers; the urgency of the next task at hand, soaking the salt out of the dinner's fish (and the sundown of Sabbath doesn't wait for me to catch up with the hour)—than of the amazements, prophecies, and promises given me seventeen years ago.

And yet I *am* keenly aware of the Giver of miracles—the breath in the child, the leaven in the bread, the salt in the fish.

Why does *the* miracle seem far away, as if it might have been a dream? The years of domesticity, the houseful of children seeded by a husband's familiar—they tempt me to think that life could never have been out of the ordinary, that the first child couldn't have been conceived any differently than the others.

The appearances—angels, shepherds, wise men of the east—did I imagine them?

I asked Joseph to dig up the gold, so I could see and touch it.

He questioned my sanity but obliged, after all the children were asleep, though our getting up in the middle of the night woke Jesus, who came out when he heard the digging. Groggy, he woke up fast when Joseph described the treasure hunt.

"See? Satisfied?"

Yes dear. Thank you.

Jesus, turning eighteen. Joseph says it's time to find him a wife, though the boy has never begged the issue as James is already, though several years younger.

Joseph says Benjamin has been by the shop now twice in a month for no real reason. He wonders if Benjamin is looking at Jesus as a prospective husband for his daughter Abigail, a nice enough girl I suppose, though there's not a one in town who would perfectly suit me.

Though a man must find a wife and not a woman a husband (as the sons of Adam search, search their missing rib), the betrothal negotiations are a study in maneuvers, like the history of two armies each trying to set up the next strategic move (one hopes for a kinder purpose).

Yesterday Benjamin boldly asked Joseph if he intended to disgrace himself and die without making provision for grandchildren. It was as close to an offer to negotiate a marriage proposal as one would ever hear. Joseph made no commitments but slammed no doors.

He tells me he thinks this is the right match. The one we should propose.

I think we should not say another word to Benjamin before discussing the matter with Jesus, who will not admit there's any truth in James's taunts that he's sweet on Abigail.

Today Joseph will ask Jesus if he will have Abigail, assuming we can come to an acceptable agreement with Benjamin, which shouldn't be difficult.

Have I seen Joseph this angry since he was negotiating details of his own marriage?

When asked, Jesus refused to have anything to do with serious talk of betrothal. Benjamin's accusations of Joseph fueled Joseph's of Jesus. Will the family be disgraced? Will he refuse to carry the responsibility inherent in Jewish manhood?

It remains a standoff. Joseph fears for his business, should Benjamin take affront and choose to malign us—digging up old stories and reminding us and anyone who will listen that "our kind" cannot afford to be so particular. . .

All too soon our own Elizabeth will be of age. I cringe at the thought of having to beg a bargain.

Before dinner James was boasting that he had out-run Jesus, racing from here to the edge of town. James *is* going to be the bigger and stronger of the two.

This was James's first taste of being number one, outshining his older brother. I let him gloat.

Jesus challenged him to a rematch tomorrow.

Today Jesus won the contest, but he won't keep his standing for long.

At the synagogue I watch: It's clearly James who is making eyes at giggling Abigail. It is the match we will propose.

"Joseph . . . before your father came knocking at my father's door . . . did you have clear intentions of who you wished to marry . . . or were 'we' your father's idea?"

He laughed. "Wouldn't you say 'we' were the *Lord's* idea?"

Memory: Father whitewashing the house a few days before he and Father Jacob signed our betrothal covenant. I was standing behind him. He turned around and said, "Mary, he's no Solomon, but better to have a bridled horse than a wild one."

I wasn't even sure what he was talking about.

The air is still heavy between Joseph and Jesus.

PART 8

Departures

Sighing comes to me instead of food;
  my groans pour out like water.
What I feared has come upon me;
  what I dreaded has happened to me.

—*Job*

Love Poem for Dying Joseph

A virgin warmed David as I warm you,
slipping blue from my hold
like light from dusk.
I pray on your shallow breath and wait out
the night pleading an angel break in
and grant us ten more years.
A virgin warmed David as I warm you,
slipping blue from my hold
like dark from dawn.

He's gone. Near dawn his breath just grew more and more irregular. At the end I kept waiting for another, not wanting to believe there wouldn't be one.

Neighbors have brought in bread and figs . . . and water. I am so tired. I've had so little sleep. My voice is raspy and my throat sore. The road from here to the grave outside of town was longer than the road to Jerusalem. I have no memory of Jesus' firstborn prayers over his father's body.

He who makes peace in the high places, may He make peace for us and all Israel. Amen.

There's a new rhythm to the day. With every exhale I tell myself to let him go. Let him go. Let go of twenty-four years of married life.

If I could only hold my breath there and be content. But the pain of his absence sweeps back in when my chest involuntarily rises, reaching for life or is it love?

To everything there is a season. A time to breathe in, a time to breathe out. A time to hold on, a time to let go.

Look at King David's mourning: His young son dies. He has been so distraught over the illness—fasting, praying, lying prone on the ground—that his servants fear to tell him of the death. "He may do something desperate."

Instead, hearing the news David washes, changes his clothes, worships God, and asks for food. "While the child was still alive, I fasted and wept. *Who knows? The Lord may be gracious to me and let the child live.* But the boy is dead. Can my fasting bring him back again? I will go to him, but he will not return to me."

Such a reasoned response. Acknowledging death. Claiming life. I can reach for it but it is out of my grasp.

The Wisdom: How can one be warm alone?

In Abraham's bosom. That's Jesus' comfort to me and to the younger children. He seems to get a great deal of pleasure (is he comforting himself?) in detail-

ing a scene of a great banquet where Joseph is sitting
on Abraham's right, eating delicacies the names of
which he pulls out of the air. It does get us laughing.
He gives a name. Then the kids guess if they think it's
a nut or a long green vegetable or a bread made from
dark brown grain. Sometimes he strings them out a
long time. No. No. Guess again. Sometimes he lets
them get it "right" real quick. He is a light in our dark
sorrow.

Today Jesus' guessing game was of animals and
birds that, he says, Joseph and Abraham are keepers
of. The same outlandish names. A few times they
never guessed right and he described his own fan-
cies: for instance, a furry, four-legged animal, two
strong back legs for hopping and two short front legs
for eating and running. There was more. A long thick
snaky tail and, get this, a stomach pouch for carrying
newborn babies. Such an imagination.

Poem: The Presence of His Absence
I would write it if I had the presence of mind . . .

I think I've become preoccupied with feeding the
household. Eat. Eat. Tomorrow you may die. Vain
attempts at trying to feel as if I have some control.

There is a motherly quality in this fatherless boy. His
mere presence but also his word have the effect of
pulling thorns of grief from my flesh, not all at once

but one by one. Each day I can sense a place raw yesterday has healed over, though how many spindles remain?

Sister Mary—with Clopas and her brood—came back down today from Cana to offer comfort. I have missed her and wish she were closer. I asked James and Abigail for dinner. There was laughter in the house, especially by Clopas, teasing that his Young Joseph would prove his manhood before Jesus.

It is not a subject we family—Mother, James, I—often broach. Gibes from customers he sloughs off, but I didn't know how he'd respond to the stick-em-up spirit of an old playmate.

So how did he react? As if it were a game, as if they were still ten years old. The two went out in the yard, wrestled for ten minutes, and came back in looking for something to drink and reminiscing some schoolhouse escapade I'd never heard anything about.

Years back I asked Jesus who he most admired in the Scriptures. He said Moses and I wondered then if his opinion would change. So I asked again today.

"Abraham."

"Why?"

"Because he was willing to give up his son."

"From all appearances you'll never have a son."

It was unnecessary. It just slipped out. I shouldn't have said it, so I suppose I deserved his hit: "But you do."

Why did the One who never slumbers create "in His image" us who must?

Our Simon is thirteen and this Sabbath reading and giving his commentary in the service. For months Jesus has been drilling him on the Torah as if this boy were his own firstborn and his own knowledge of the Scriptures were on the line. Well, admit it: From the start Jesus was more of a father to this orphan than Joseph.

Troublesome dream: The family was traveling to Jerusalem. Passover. The road was overgrown first with nettles, then with thistles, and eventually with thorn bushes so thick our clothing was shredded and we were cut and stabbed head to foot.

Oh that I had Patriarch Joseph here to interpret.

Zechariah's John is calling us a generation of vipers, snakes. I suppose I should think this over before making judgments, however . . . To put it politely, where is the boy's respect? It's a grace his father is dead so he doesn't have to go to the temple and face the scowls of the other priests. The disgrace—or honor—of a child is always the disgrace—or honor—of the parent.

The boy never seemed one of us. Called to be one of the wild prophets, an Amos or Jeremiah. I can live with the rantings of the wild ones, as long as accounts of their words and deeds are inked in the holy scrolls. It was long ago. Not here and now. Yes, they were living in a wicked and perverse generation. They'd turned to false gods. But we? The prayers of God's people rise from this land like early-morning steam off the lake.

I suppose I could name a viper or two. But a whole generation?

Another birthday.

The oil no longer works to keep my hands soft like sand on the riverbank. The skin cracks now, like sun-caked mud, like Mother's when she was no longer young.

The rabbis say we can blame these signs of aging on Abraham who foolishly asked that he be distinguishable from grown, handsome son Isaac. Beware lest your wishes be granted: hoary hair, loose, leathery skin, veins bulged and looking like purple worms.

Forty-four years today. Old. Not so old. Old enough.

At the Purim service I always listen for one line in Queen Esther's story. It's Mordecai's nudge that bridges Esther's past and future: Who knows but that you have come to the kingdom for such a time as this?

Every year when I hear them the words quicken my spirit in a bittersweet manner. This Purim was no different.

The heavenly visitors, the miracle conception—they were real promises of a blessed future. I stand assured: This manchild (my manchild, and therefore I) was sent to the kingdom for such a time as this. And yet I can never grasp a hold of that "such

a time," since every small-town Nazareth day—him
in the shop, me chopping onions and seeding melons,
a generation being born, a generation dying—passes
as uneventful as the one before.

I'm going to ask Jesus if he has any more clarity
than I.

He says he will come into his own soon, very soon.
"You won't understand," he said, no—he warned.
"I'll have to leave." He tried to lighten things up.
"Remember, you used to ask me my favorite charac-
ter of the Scriptures? Ask me now."

I obliged.

"Isaiah, the poet preoccupied with the servant."

But Mother, you don't understand. I thought I might
have to hear it for five years. It now has been—what,
fifteen?—and I'm still counting.

And first thing this morning he said that he would
leave the morning after Sabbath—to find and talk to
Zechariah's John, walking the banks of the river in
Judea.

Well, when will you be home?

"Young Joseph's wedding. It's in, what, two
months? I'll be back for it. But not for long."

What about your work orders?

"James can handle them and he can handle Simon,
who just needs a steadying hand. It won't be long
before he's ready to carry a full load."

Well what about your provisions? How much shall
I pack for you?

"Enough figs and nuts for three days."

When you come back "not for long," then what?

"Mother . . ." I knew I didn't want to hear what would follow. "I can't thank you enough for your care. Your willingness. Your sheltering wing. But I'm a grown man. You'd be celebrating if I were leaving you to cleave to a wife; for that reason you would have been willing to let go ten years ago. It's time. I have to talk to John, then I'll know more. He has a message for me. "

I don't remember ever showing anyone anything I've written in these pages. But today, after pondering yesterday's conversation, I showed Jesus the childbirth poem that came with the twins' delivery.

He stared at it a long time. "Thank you, Mother."

Do you want the Gentiles' gold? Dig it up and take it. It's yours. I'll show you right where it is.

"No, keep it. You may need it."

Simon struggled to hold back tears when Jesus left. If I read him right he's feeling sorrow but also anger at being deserted, abandoned again. I wonder how things will change between the two—fatherless both.

I'll have to talk to James; it won't be long before we must consider a wife for Simon. He's a restless one who needs a bridle.

I was forced to let go of Joseph. Did that make letting go of the children easier—or harder?

Maybe easier. In their absence I know that a piece of them remains behind.

Our sex is much maligned for the weakness of a few. The rabbis imagine the Name's thoughts upon creating Eve: "I will not make her from man's head, lest she be arrogant. Nor from his eye, lest she be wanton-eyed. Nor from his ear, lest she be an eavesdropper. Nor from his neck, lest she be insolent. Nor from his mouth, lest she be a tattler. Nor from his heart, lest she be the envious sort. Nor from his hand, lest she be a meddler. Nor from his foot, lest she be a gadabout. I will form her from a chaste portion, a rib, so she will be chaste."

But they do not stop there. They continue, enumerating these faults as found in our mothers. Despite His desire for a chaste, honorable companion for man, woman has all the weakness He was trying to avoid: The haughty daughters of Zion who walked with outstretched necks and flirtatious eyes. Sarah, eavesdropper. Miriam, bearer of accusations against Moses. Rachel, jealous of her sister Leah. Eve, who plucked the forbidden fig. Dinah, gadabout that she was.

No, do not grieve. Choose to consider the stories of other foremothers and ponder why they are acclaimed for their faith, courage, even conniving, when it is for our people's cause:

Rebekah, scheming to grant the birthright to her younger son.

Tamar, disguising herself and by trickery claiming her rights from Judah.

Jochebed and the midwives, resisting the king's decree and saving a son.

Rahab, bargaining safety for safety and lying to keep her word.

Ruth, staking a claim on Boaz.

Deborah, mustering and leading a victorious army.

Abigail, betraying her drunk husband.

Diplomatic Judith, tricking and beheading sleeping Holofernes.

Queen Esther, saving the kingdom in more feminine fashion.

What do you make of this? A wily group generally praised for doing what needed to be done, for rising to the occasion.

Only two days until Young Joseph's wedding. Will Jesus come and go up to Cana with the family? Or maybe meet us there?

He isn't here and we leave for the wedding early in the morning. Disappointed: I was hoping he would come home, sleep under my roof, eat my stew, walk up with us.

First night in Cana: Yes, he's here—and with a train of robust and rowdy fishermen he's picked up. (Oh, be kind. Two of them are your own nephews, Salome's James and John.) But he's hardly robust. He's half starved, a shadow of what he once was. Eight weeks away from my table and look at him. It's worse than locusts and honey, which would keep some flesh on his bones.

And his eyes. He's ten years older than when he left.

He says he had to fast, forty days in the wild. John had recommended a group of caves. Not to worry.

I couldn't help it. I wanted answers: Are you . . . and John . . . living off the land . . . one of the wild prophets . . . like Jeremiah? Such a future you found in the desert . . . the promised future?

"The future is full of miracles, and my work is kinder than John's. The crowds are going to dance like wedding guests.

"Come on, Mother, it's time to celebrate, which is what I'm here to do."

And the music plays on. Clopas insists we stay on past the Sabbath. He's obviously enjoying his role as host, maybe showing off his prosperity (I can give a better party than you), maybe displaying his intemperance (I can hold more wine than you).

Actually, I'm seeing signs that the whole celebration is not as well organized as it should be. At one point this evening one of the waiters—supposedly under the eye of the bride's uncle who is partying more than supervising—was asking me for direction.

I'll try to keep an eye on things tomorrow, but even when you're family you have to watch and not step in and try to manage someone else's affairs.

It was water. Six huge pots of wine—from water.

"A future full of miracles." "I'll come into my own very soon." "I'm here to celebrate." When the waiter caught my eye (Help. We're out of wine. What do we do now?), all the phrases came together in my mind. It was time for me—well, him actually, but I had to present the opportunity—to rise to the occasion. Like Rebekah. Tamar. Jochebed . . . the mothers.

"Jesus, Clopas doesn't know it but he's run out of wine." (Do something.)

"Woman," (not *Mother*; a kind but distanced *Woman*), "you're out of line dragging me into this. It's none of my concern. Don't push me." That's what he said, but I could read his eyes, which said, "All right. I'll never feel ready, but, all right, I'll jump. I'll do something."

What was I expecting? I don't even know. Did he know? Did he know what he was capable of?

When the wine was served out, when the bride's uncle handed a cup to Clopas and Young Joseph, he asked why they'd held back such a fine vintage. Clopas just smiled—neither confirming nor denying some reasoned explanation.

The story—water to wine—eventually spread through the crowd, by way of the fishermen. I watched Jesus who was watching reactions—didn't say a word to draw attention to himself.

Jesus says he is heading to Capernaum on the lake, and I will take the opportunity to go up and visit Sister Salome, then head home.

Dream, first night back in Nazareth: No angel this time. Jesus was standing in the doorway as if he'd just come in from the shop. He was smiling but intent, focusing all his attention on me. "Mother, you were chosen like a prophet, like weeping Jeremiah lamenting the woes of the kingdom. I pray for you.

"Now you—weave like Samuel's Hannah and pray for me, the loan that was lent to you."

What this was about the weaving I don't know for sure. But I'll do it. I'll spin, then weave, the longest threads I ever have—a rich man's cloth that will make a seamless robe—and I'll dye it dark brown, walnut.

It will take me how long?—too long—but with every woolen thread pushed in ordered line, I'll speak the boy's name, pleading a father's loving-kindness on this my departed son.